"You're the Last Man
I'd Care to Be Alone With!"

Kelly snapped. "You're nine-tenths machine. You have a computer terminal for a heart."

"A computer terminal, is it?" Jake growled. "Let's see how much of me is made of machinery, shall we?"

Kelly was unable to struggle as his mouth descended on hers. Her senses whirled in a kaleidoscope of reactions as Jake explored further.

"You *are* a witch," Jake muttered thickly against her lips. "How many men have kissed you this way?"

LINDA WISDOM

counts writing chief among her many interests. The world of imagination has always been real to her, and with her novels she is able to bring everyone's dreams of love and romance to life.

Dear Reader:

I'd like to take this opportunity to thank you for all your support and encouragement of Silhouette Romances.

Many of you write in regularly, telling us what you like best about Silhouette, which authors are your favorites. This is a tremendous help to us as we strive to publish the best contemporary romances possible.

All the romances from Silhouette Books are for you, so enjoy this book and the many stories to come. I hope you'll continue to share your thoughts with us, and invite you to write to us at the address below:

Karen Solem
Editor-in-Chief
Silhouette Books
P.O. Box 769
New York, N.Y. 10019

LINDA WISDOM
Dreams from the Past

Silhouette *Romance*
Published by Silhouette Books New York
America's Publisher of Contemporary Romance

Other Silhouette Books by Linda Wisdom

Dancer in the Shadows
Fourteen Karat Beauty
Bright Tomorrow
A Man with Doubts

 SILHOUETTE BOOKS, a Simon & Schuster Division of
GULF & WESTERN CORPORATION
1230 Avenue of the Americas, New York, N.Y. 10020

ISBN: 0-671-57166-4

First Silhouette Books printing August, 1982

10 9 8 7 6 5 4 3 2 1

Map by Tony Ferrara

America's Publisher of Contemporary Romance

Printed in the U.S.A.

Dreams from
the Past

Chapter One

The hospital corridor was deserted as the young woman wearing a fur coat hurried toward one of the rooms at the end of the hall. Spying a man lounging against the wall, she halted in front of him, an anxious expression on her face.

"Kyle, how is he?" she asked breathlessly, touching the man's arm.

"Not good," he replied grimly. "That's why the doctor asked us to come. He doesn't think Dad will last through the night. This last attack was a bad one."

The young woman pulled off her tan-colored fur hat and unbuttoned her coat, shrugging it off. Long, wavy honey-colored hair cascaded freely to her shoulders, framing her heart-shaped face with its luminous turquoise eyes. Her oatmeal-colored wool dress clung to her slender curves, ending just above her dark brown suede boots. A dark brown soft leather belt hugged her trim waist, and a gold pendant was her only jewelry. Even with the evidence of strain and tension on her face she was still breathtakingly beautiful. Her expressive eyes shimmered with unshed tears at the thought of the vital, warm, and loving man, her father, lying helpless in a hospital bed.

"Kelly." The young man took her out of her thoughts. "Dad's been asking for you for the past hour. He wants to talk to you—alone."

Kelly smiled fondly at her twin brother, Kyle. When they were together, their easy grace and unusual coloring always earned them a second glance from passersby. She moved slowly to the door, turned the handle, and walked quietly into the hospital room. Her heart sank as she gazed down at the dark-haired man lying waxen against the white sheets.

"Hello, princess," he said feebly, holding out a hand. "I thought you'd be in Jamaica by now, lying in the sun and breaking all the men's hearts."

"Now, why would I want to go to Jamaica when I can stay here with my favorite man?" Kelly asked lightly, sinking down into the chair next to the bed. "I thought you had promised us to stay away from hospitals for a while. I was hoping you would come to Jamaica with me so you could lie in the sun yourself and get away from all of this horrible snow."

Ross James viewed his daughter with loving eyes. "To this day I still wonder if the hospital made a mistake with you and Kyle," he murmured. "No one else on either side of the family has eyes that color."

"You shouldn't talk so much," she chided. "Not when I'm finally sitting down with a captive audience and can chatter away to my heart's content."

Her father smiled, knowing only too well that his daughter could never be described as an idle chatterbox. "I have something to say; then you can talk my ear off, if you'd like," he told her. "First, why don't you bring me that manila envelope on that table over there."

Standing up, Kelly walked with fluid grace to the table her father had indicated and looked down at a dog-eared and discolored envelope. Picking it up, she carried it back and handed it to her father.

"Family secrets?" she asked with a smile.

"More like ancient secrets, considering your tender years," Ross replied. He struggled to sit up, and his daughter hurriedly assisted him. His expression was unreadable as he looked down at the envelope in his hands. "As you know, during World War Two I convalesced in an army hospital in New Zealand. That land-mine explosion had done quite a bit of damage, and I was laid up for a long time. But there's sonething I never told anyone. Until now." Kelly sat quietly, waiting for her father to continue.

"During that painful period when I was learning to walk again, I was not the easiest patient to deal with, I can assure you," Ross said wryly. "In fact, the only thing that kept me going was a saucy nurse's aide who worked in the hospital several days a week." His eyes were looking far away into the past. "Maureen Kilpatrick . . . Irish from the top of her glossy dark head to the tips of her toes.

9

When I was finally released from the hospital, I spent my leave in New Zealand with Maureen, and I fell in love with her. As far as I was concerned, being with her was the next best thing to being in heaven. It didn't take long for me to realize I wanted to spend the rest of my life with her, and I asked her to marry me."

"Did something happen to her, Daddy?" Kelly asked in a low voice, laying her hand on her father's arm.

"No." He sighed. "Well, not exactly. It also didn't take long for us to discover we had equally stubborn natures. We had one foolish argument when neither of us would give in to the other. We said words that couldn't be taken back. Maureen went away to her family's home, and I was shipped back to the States to receive my medical discharge." Kelly sat quietly as her father paused for a moment. "When I returned home, I realized how silly our argument had been and wrote to Maureen, begging her to reconsider and marry me. I loved her too deeply to give her up. And for six months I waited vainly for her reply. When I didn't receive one by then, I figured that she had only thought of me as a wartime romance and had already forgotten me. It wasn't long afterward that I met your mother and married her." He shifted uncomfortably in his bed, a spasm of pain crossing his features. "It was then that I finally received Maureen's letter. For some insane reason my letter had been delayed in the mails, and so had her reply. She wrote that she loved me very much and still wanted to marry me."

"Oh, Daddy," Kelly whispered, gripping his hand.

Ross smiled faintly. "I didn't know what to do. I loved your mother, but I still loved Maureen, too. The hardest thing I ever did was to write to her about my marriage. I was feeling pretty low as it was, what with the war in full swing and me home, still suffering from a game leg. Five months later I received a short note saying that she had married a cattle rancher and was moving to New South Wales. She wished me the best of luck with my marriage. The rest you know. Michael was born; then, some years later, you and Kyle came along."

"You never forgot her, though, did you?" Kelly asked softly.

"Maureen was very special to me." Ross smiled. "I kept track of her through the years because, for whatever reason, I hated to lose sight of her completely. Her husband died five years ago. She has two sons; one is in charge of the ranch now, and doing very well."

"Why didn't you contact her? Go see her? Mother was gone; there wouldn't have been any harm in it now."

"I was afraid Maureen wouldn't see me, or, worse yet, would have forgotten me," he said wryly. "A lot of years have gone by. But lately I've thought more and more about her. That's why I want you to do something for me." He opened the envelope and pulled out a photograph, handing it to Kelly. "Maureen," Ross said simply.

Kelly studied the black-and-white photo, which showed a smiling young woman of nineteen or twenty looking up at a younger version of her father in an army uniform. The expressions on their faces told her everything else she needed to know. They had loved each other deeply.

"There are also some letters Maureen wrote to me. She couldn't bear the thought of my not receiving mail while I was in the hospital, so she would write me every night. I kept them all. I also have her present address in there." Ross took the photograph back from his daughter. "Kelly, I'm asking you to take these letters back to Maureen. They'll show her that I never forgot her, even after all these years."

"Do you really think that's a good idea?" Kelly asked hesitantly. "It's been so long. Perhaps you'd be better off burning them, or just mailing them back to her."

"No, I want them returned to her in person," he said firmly. "Kelly, I'm not just asking you; I'm begging you to do this for me. We both know there's no way I'll be able to go there myself. Go to Australia, see Maureen, and give her letters back to her."

"Wouldn't Kyle be better at this?" she asked. "He's the diplomat in the family, not I."

Ross gave a faint smile. "Kyle may have a way with words, but he's also very fickle when it comes to the subject of women and romance. He'd never understand how I feel about this."

Kelly returned his smile, knowing all too

much about the long succession of girlfriends her twin had had in the past few years.

"Please, Kelly." Ross's eyes pleaded with her. "Go to her. See her."

"Well, I'll see what I can do." She reluctantly accepted the envelope her father held out to her. Silently, she wondered if she was doing the right thing in bringing up memories that were almost forty years old.

Some hours later, Kelly was looking out at the falling snow from a window in her father's small house. Her cheeks bore traces of recent tears as she thought that he would never again see his home, whose rooms he had filled with antiques and fireplaces . . . and his own irreplaceable warmth.

"I wonder what we should do now." Kyle's quiet voice interrupted her thoughts. She turned to look at her twin.

"We can't think of ourselves now, Kyle," Kelly replied.

Kyle flopped down carelessly in a large chair, draping one long leg over the arm. His honey-blond hair, usually so carefully styled, showed signs of the agitated fingers that had raked through the thick strands, yet his cream-colored slacks and navy V-necked sweater were as impeccable as they had been when he put them on eighteen hours earlier. Although his features were definitely masculine, he was almost a mirror image of Kelly, his large, expressive, deep turquoise eyes framed with dark, thick lashes just as hers were. Kyle picked up a magazine and flipped idly through the pages. He stopped at one page and flicked a finger against the shiny paper.

"What about this, sister dear?" He arched a questioning eyebrow at her.

Kelly walked over and picked up the magazine, gazing down at the picture Kyle had pointed out, a picture that was so familar to her. The early evening sky formed a backdrop for a winged horse, flying off toward the rising moon, while a young man and woman, dressed in the colorful clothing popular with the disco set, walked along the beach—Kelly and Kyle, looking as if they didn't have a care in the world.

"'Pegasus for today.'" She took in the bright yellow lettering at the bottom of the page and read the caption aloud. "It's amazing how something as silly as this can sell clothing all over the world."

"*We* are what sells those clothes," Kyle drawled lazily. "People buy them hoping they'll look like us."

"Conceited lout," Kelly said affectionately. She dispassionately viewed her reflection in the ornate mirror that hung on the wall behind her. There was no vanity in her gaze. Kelly knew she was beautiful, but she also knew that outer beauty wasn't as meaningful as inner beauty, no matter how many clothes the former was capable of selling.

Her honey-colored hair was skillfully cut to frame her face before falling past her shoulders in a careless style, but it was still long enough to be coiled back and out of the way in a smooth knot. Her skin was golden, and her brightly shining turquoise eyes were her trademark.

"Now, as to this request of Dad's, you're not really going to Australia, are you?" Kyle asked. "After all, all that happened almost forty years ago. It would be a fool's errand. Who says this woman even remembers Dad?"

"Oh, I think she does." Kelly picked up the photograph she had been carrying with her all evening and studied the smiling couple. Her eyes shimmered with tears as she thought again about the loss of the man who had guided her life for so many years. For Ross James had also been Kelly and Kyle's business manager. When their modeling careers began flourishing, he had taken over the business end, expertly managing and investing their earnings. "Did you call Michael?"

"Yes. He's taking the morning flight." Kyle stood up and stretched tiredly. "I'm going to get a few hours' sleep." He looked toward his sister with the uncanny perception they had always shared. "Kelly?"

She turned and saw the expression on her brother's face, then walked slowly toward him and put her arms around him, laying her head against his shoulder. "Oh, Kyle." Her voice quavered with unshed tears. "Daddy's gone, and we're all alone. What are we going to do?" At that moment she sounded more like a ten-year-old child than a young woman of twenty-four.

"We'll do all right, kid." Kyle had always acted the part of the older brother, although there were only a few minutes between them. "Why don't you get some rest, too. I'll worry about picking Michael up at the airport."

Later, lying in bed, Kelly found herself unable to sleep. Thoughts tumbled chaotically through her mind as she recalled her father's request. On impulse, she sat up and switched on a lamp, then picked up the manila envelope from the bedside table. Opening it, she drew out several of the letters. After hesitating only briefly, she unfolded the sheets of pale blue stationery and began to read.

Totally engrossed, Kelly was still poring over the letters when the darkness outside turned to gray dawn. Putting down the last letter, Kelly knew she had to travel to Australia and meet Maureen Cassidy, once Maureen Kilpatrick.

A month later Kelly boarded a jet for Sydney, Australia, Kyle's protests, which she had ignored, still in her mind.

"This is ridiculous, Kel," he had argued earlier while watching his sister carefully fold clothing and place it in her suitcases. "Surely Dad didn't expect you to go through with this crazy scheme. Besides, you had a trip to Jamaica all planned, and you've been looking forward to that for months. Not to mention the fact that our contracts come up for renewal in six weeks."

"Why don't you come with me?" she had suggested, ignoring his arguments. "We've never had a chance to visit that part of the world. We could have a lot of fun."

"I'm saying you shouldn't go, not asking to go along with you. We may be each other's best friend, but we can also be wet blankets for any relationship the other one may be trying to form."

Kelly had looked up with surprise, a smile curving her lips. "Kyle, have you met someone?" Her question had brought a flush to her brother's face. "You have, haven't you? 'Fess up."

"I'm not sure," he had answered honestly. "But I'd like to find out. No offense, but it *is* easier without a sister on my heels. Even so, I just don't feel right about your going all the way to Australia. Something could happen to you, and I'd be on the other side of the world, unable to help you out."

"I'll be fine," Kelly had assured him. "You just concentrate on yourself for a while; you know I'm on your side all the way. You'll have nothing to worry about. What could possibly happen to me over there that I couldn't handle?"

Sitting back in her seat, Kelly smiled to herself as the city below grew smaller as the jet gained altitude. She didn't feel entirely confident about her mission, despite what she had told Kyle, but she felt that she could make the best of it and come off fine. She leaned back and tried to put the immediate past and the impending future from her mind.

Even though she was a seasoned traveler, Kelly was exhausted when the jet landed in Sydney. She gratefully shrugged off her fur coat in the heat of the summer sun. How

17

strange, she thought, to have the seasons so switched around. After clearing customs and collecting her luggage, Kelly hailed a taxi, glad that she had made her hotel reservations in advance. It was not long before she was installed in her hotel suite and collapsed gratefully in the bed for a long nap.

The next morning Kelly was up early, eager to do some sightseeing. But first she took out the address her father had scrawled on a piece of paper and sat down at the writing table with several sheets of hotel stationery in front of her. After an hour spent chewing her pen and sighing in frustration, Kelly finished her note and sealed the addressed envelope, ready for mailing.

During the several days she spent waiting for her letter to be received, Kelly enjoyed herself traveling about the city and taking in the sights, including Sydney's famous Opera House, which was known for its ultramodern architecture and fine acoustics. Everywhere she went, classical old buildings were interspersed with modern structures of granite and concrete.

Taking the ferry to cross the harbor, Kelly visited Tauranga Zoological Park and Aquarium, making sure that her camera was loaded with film; she wanted to have plenty of pictures to remember this trip by. She enjoyed wandering about the seventy acres of bushland and bright gardens, taking pictures like any typical tourist. She saw kangaroos and wallabies, the small black scrubland kangaroos. She was surprised to find the female kangaroos so gentle that she could pet them, unlike the male, or buck, who was very protective of his family.

But Kelly lost her heart to the cuddly, woolly koalas. Picking one up in her arms so she could have her picture taken with it, she could understand why the lovable koala was so popular with adults and children alike as the furry animal cuddled close to her.

"You're definitely much better looking than my brother and not half as temperamental," she informed the koala with a straight face. "Perhaps you'd like to take up a modeling career. How would you feel about wearing jeans?"

Kelly spent another day at the Art Gallery of New South Wales in the Domain, enjoying the chance to study the large collection of Australian paintings and statuary in addition to the collection of foreign artists' work. Everywhere she went she found the people friendly and helpful, and easily charmed by her blond beauty and ready smile.

She rapidly discovered how much she enjoyed the easy life as she walked or rode buses through the city, content to take her time in looking at things, glad not to have a hectic schedule to follow. The closest she came to entering the working world was watching office workers playing cricket, the English form of baseball, during their breaks.

Kelly also spent her time indulging in what her brother called the favorite pastime of every woman: shopping. Wandering through Martin Place and the principal shopping streets, all named for British sovereigns or prime ministers, she found beautiful wool skirts and sweaters, finely made leather goods, and delicately formed jewelry, all of which delighted her. Since the opal was her birthstone, Kelly especially enjoyed finding the gem in varied shades she hadn't ever imagined possible. There were even beautiful black opals, which she purchased in the form of a pendant, several rings and bracelets, and two pairs of earrings.

"I'll definitely be renewing my contract," she muttered to herself as she signed over several traveler's checks to the jeweler.

Kelly was amused to find American fashion magazines on the newsstands, complete with pictures of her and Kyle. She had almost forgotten about the immense popularity of Pegasus Designs.

"Miss James, I have a telegram for you," the desk clerk informed her when she returned to the hotel late one afternoon after a full and tiring day of sightseeing.

Kelly flashed him a sunny smile as she accepted the white envelope. She waited until she had reached her suite before opening the envelope and drawing out the contents. A frown creased her forehead as she read the words; then anger took over.

Miss James,

I don't know what the reasoning is behind this farce, but it won't work. Don't trouble yourself by coming out to Acacia Tree. You won't be welcome.

J. T. Cassidy

"Of all the nerve," Kelly muttered to herself. "If this J. T. Cassidy thinks this is going to keep me away, he's got another think coming." Remembering her initial reluctance to come to Australia, Kelly realized how differently she now felt. After examining the photograph her father had given her and reading the letters, Kelly had known she had to meet Maureen Cassidy—and this cable only added fuel to the fire. Picking up the phone, she spoke to the front desk and arranged transport to the Outback region of New South Wales. Then she began packing her clothes as if preparing for battle.

Kelly continued to be fascinated by the switch in seasons. She had left snow and ice behind in New York City and found summer weather here, with warm sunshine and greenery. But even in summer the Outback looked forbidding as she gazed through the window of her small plane. After she landed at the airfield in Bathurst, Kelly arranged to rent a car for the remainder of her journey. In deference to the heat, she wore slim-fitting jeans and a print cotton shirt, with her hair pinned up on top of her head for coolness. Studying her map, she began the last leg of her trip.

When Kelly arrived in Canowindra, the town closest to the Cassidy homestead, she checked into the hotel and did some exploring on her own. Using her beauty and charm to their fullest, Kelly was soon able to send word of her arrival to Mrs. Maureen Cassidy by means of one of the stockmen who worked for the Cassidys. She had already decided against using the telephone, afraid she might not reach the right party if J. T. Cassidy had anything to say about it.

Feeling tired after her trip, Kelly headed back to the hotel that evening wanting only a shower and bed. She pushed open the door of her room, then uttered a cry of alarm on seeing a man's broad figure seated in the chair near the window.

"Miss James?" His voice was deep and husky.

"Who are you?" Kelly demanded. "And how did you get into my room?"

"I explained to Cal that I wanted to speak to you in private. One of my men gave me your message for Maureen Cassidy." He stubbed his cigarette out in a nearby ashtray, not bothering to get to his feet. "I'm J. T. Cassidy. Jake."

"Oh?" She walked over to the dresser and leaned back against the edge. "So *you're* J. T. Cassidy. Excuse me if I'm not impressed." Her eyes were as hard as turquoise stones as she surveyed the man seated before her. Kelly silently admitted that Jake Cassidy was handsome in a rough-hewn way. Black hair threaded with silver curled over the collar of his dark wine-colored shirt, while his deep green eyes surveyed her slim figure with insulting thoroughness. She could feel her jeans and print shirt, its tails tied below her breasts, stripped away by the merciless gaze.

"What do you hope to gain by this game of yours, Miss James?" he said at length. "Are you doing this for kicks, or are you looking for some kind of financial gain?"

If Kelly hadn't felt so angry, she would have laughed at the man's assumption that she was money hungry. "It is *not* a game, Mr. Cassidy," she said coolly. "And the last thing I need is money. I am here as a favor to my father. It was his last request that I come to see Mrs. Cassidy; it was very important to him."

"The past is dead," he said flatly. "Let it stay that way."

There had been a time when Kelly would have wholeheartedly agreed with Jake Cassidy, but not now, not after making that promise to her father and reading those letters. "I can only assume that you must be her son. But that doesn't give you the right to make her decisions for her," she taunted. "She's certainly an adult and doesn't need you to run her life for her."

"My mother is still recovering from an illness she contracted last winter," he said quietly. "I intend to see that nothing—and *no one*—upsets her. Especially a schemer like you."

Kelly turned to pick up the manila envelope and threw it on the man's lap. "Inside you will find a photograph of your mother and my father and letters your mother wrote to my father. He asked me to return them to her, to let her know he still thought of her. That what happened years ago was not entirely his own doing."

"Your letter claimed your father died recently." Jake Cassidy viewed the items on his lap dispassionately.

"I don't *claim* it; it's a fact," Kelly snapped, disliking the man more and more. "Look, this really has nothing to do with you, so why don't you just run along and—"

"You little fool," he grated, rising to his feet in one fluid motion and walking over to stand in front of her. "*Anything* concerning my mother concerns me. You come out here, with your fancy designer jeans and flashy looks, and think you can stir up the past and painful memories. Let me tell you, lady, it just won't happen."

At five foot seven, Kelly rarely had to look so far up at a man as she did at this one. Even if she had worn high heels instead of the flat-heeled sandals she had on, he would still have towered over her. She felt a moment's fear at his nearness, but refused to show it. "You can't scare me, Mr. Cassidy." Her voice was soft but determined.

Jake Cassidy clenched his fist, as if he wanted to strike her. "We'll meet again, Miss James." It sounded more like a threat than a promise. Then he was gone.

Kelly collapsed against the edge of the dresser, heaving a sigh of relief. Although he had been with her for less than ten minutes, she felt as if she had been battling the large man for several hours. Gritting her teeth, she determined not to see that man again if she could help it.

The next morning Kelly was downstairs in the dining room enjoying her second cup of coffee when she felt an eerie prickling sensation between her shoulder blades. Refusing to give in to her curiosity, she sat hunched forward, cradling her cup between her palms.

"Mind if I sit down?"

Kelly looked up in the direction of the man's harsh voice, blandly meeting his deep green eyes. "Even if I said no, you would anyway." She shrugged her shoulders as she indicated the chair across from her. "Frankly, Mr. Cassidy, despite your parting words, after our conversation last night I didn't really expect to see you again. Or are you here to order me to be out of town by sundown?" The cold, polite smile on her face by no means took the sting out of her remark.

Jake opened his mouth as if to speak, then closed it as the proprietor of the hotel approached them with a welcoming smile for Jake.

"Mornin', Jake. Get your days mixed?" He grinned. "Always thought Thursday was your day to be in town. How about a cup of coffee?"

"Fine, Cal." Jake kept his eyes on Kelly's downcast face. After a cup of steaming coffee was set before him, Jake leaned back in his chair as if he had all the time in the world.

"To be perfectly honest, I hadn't really planned on seeing you again, either. Or wanted to, for that matter."

"Oh? Then I feel extremely flattered that you're here."

"Don't. But I have an idea that you can be a very stubborn young woman and would find a way to see my mother no matter what I said. I decided I'd prefer to have you with me than against me," Jake told her.

"And what makes you think I'd agree with you on anything?" Kelly asked, looking directly at him. Without showing a flicker of interest on her face, inwardly she felt surprised at the unusual combination of jet-black hair and deep, emerald-green eyes. Especially in a man. Besides her father, she hadn't met any man she could consider a man's man. But Jake Cassidy definitely was one. "Of course, it's obvious that you're an important man in this town. You may consider what you're wearing to be everyday working clothes, but they're not what the average rancher can afford, I'm sure."

"Very observant, aren't you?" Jake flashed her a look of admiration.

"Fashion is my business. But now, what's the reason for this surprise visit?" Kelly looked at him expectantly.

"As I told you last night, my mother hasn't been well and I don't care to see her upset. But, as I said, I have an idea that, unless I have you deported from this country, you'll find a way to see her with that message from your father. So I thought that if I took you out to meet her, with your promise not to mention your father, you'd understand my reason and go home again without saying anything." Jake leaned forward in his chair, linking his hands together on top of the table. "Will you agree to that?"

"Do I have a choice?"

He slowly shook his head.

Kelly didn't hesitate. "Give me five minutes." She rose to her feet, pushing back her chair. "I'm sure you'd prefer me to present a more dignified impression to your mother." She gestured toward her jeans and T-shirt. "I promise not to do anything foolish," she said sarcastically.

Jake's eyes narrowed dangerously at her sarcasm.

Kelly hurried upstairs to change into a powder-blue gauzy dress belted tightly around her slim waist, then quickly pinned her hair on top of her head in a neat coil. After a light application of makeup and a spray of cologne, she picked up her purse and left her room. Jake Cassidy was waiting at the foot of the stairs. She could read nothing in his expression as she stood before him.

"If you don't mind . . . ?" Jake held out his hand, his sharp green eyes on Kelly's purse.

"Trusting soul, aren't you?" she mocked him, handing over the bag.

Jake snapped open the clasp and scanned the contents before handing it back to her. Then he gestured outside toward a dusty Land-Rover.

During the drive, Kelly glanced covertly at

her silent companion. "Tell me something. How are you going to explain me to your mother?" she asked him.

"You were out for a drive. Your car broke down, and I offered to take you to my place before taking you back into town." She was sure he had thought it out carefully in advance.

The warm morning sun streaming in through the windshield lulled Kelly into a drowsy state. Mentally slapping herself awake, she looked out the window at the surrounding countryside.

"When do we reach your land?" she finally asked.

"We've been on it for the past half hour."

Kelly turned, looking at him with surprise. "How large is your ranch?"

"Out here we call them stations," Jake explained. "Ours is eighty thousand acres."

"*Eighty thousand?*" Her voice ended as a squeak.

"In this country, Miss James, that's a pretty standard size for a station."

"You're a hard man, Mr. Cassidy." Kelly shifted away from him as she changed the subject. "Cold and hard. Is your mother like you?"

"My mother is the warmest, most loving woman around." Jake's words were clipped and evenly spaced.

Chastened, Kelly looked back out the window. If it weren't for her curiosity about meeting the woman who had been so important to her father at one time, she would have demanded to be taken back to town that moment.

The Land-Rover bumped over a number of cattle guards before eventually pulling up in front of a sprawling one-story house, exotic flowers blooming brightly against the white exterior. Kelly looked around with interest as Jake assisted her out of the Land-Rover.

"If I hear you, or hear *of* you, saying one word about your father, I'll strangle you myself," Jake said through clenched teeth.

"I wouldn't doubt it one bit," Kelly replied sweetly, in an undertone.

At the sound of a door opening, she looked up to see a woman walking out onto the porch. She was tall, with a heavy sprinkling of gray in hair as dark as Jake's.

"Mother, this is Kelly James, an American here on vacation. Her car broke down on the main road, so I thought I'd bring her back here to cool off before taking her into town," Jake lied smoothly. "Miss James, I'd like you to meet my mother, Maureen Cassidy." Kelly was surprised to see the affection and warmth in the man's eyes as he gazed at his mother.

"I'm very pleased to meet you, Mrs. Cassidy." She smiled. "I hope I'm not any trouble."

"Of course not," the older woman replied. "We always enjoy having visitors. I am surprised, though. Isn't this part of New South Wales a bit off the beaten path for a tourist?"

"I decided to see as much of your beautiful country as I could," Kelly explained.

Once inside the large living room, Kelly

noticed the comfortable furniture upholstered in muted tones. Maureen Cassidy excused herself for a moment, saying she'd return with cool drinks.

"Are you staying, Jake?" she asked her son when she paused for a moment in the doorway.

"No. I'm going to call the garage to pick up Miss James's car," he told her, his eyes glancing at Kelly in silent warning. She merely smiled at him with an unreadable expression on her face. "Then I want to check on a few things in the barn." He left the room.

It was a few moments before Maureen returned with a pitcher and two glasses on a tray. "What part of America do you come from, Miss James?"

"Oh, please call me Kelly. I come from New York City."

"Have you always lived there? I hear all the time how people move around so much over there."

"I was born in Seattle, Washington, then moved to New York a few years ago because of my work."

"What an unusual necklace." Maureen leaned forward to inspect the silver chain and charm around Kelly's neck. "It's a winged horse, isn't it? A Pegasus." Her eyes, the same deep shade of green as Jake's, lit up in recognition. "Of course! I've seen pictures of you in fashion magazines. You're usually with a man who resembles you."

"My twin brother," Kelly explained.

"Well, I never thought I'd meet a famous

model." The older woman's face broke out in a pleased smile. "Will you be doing any modeling while you're out here?"

"No. As your son said, this is just a vacation for me. Since I'd never been to Australia, I thought I'd try something new."

Kelly found the time passing quickly and pleasurably. Maureen Cassidy was a warm and gracious hostess. Kelly could easily see why her father had fallen in love with her. Her quiet self-assurance was something he would admire in a woman.

"You must tell me about your job," Maureen told her. "I'm sure it must be very exciting to wear all of those beautiful clothes and travel around so much."

"I just wish that was all there was to it," Kelly said wryly, then suddenly switched the subject. "You're not from around here, are you? You don't seem to have the same accent everyone else that I've heard has."

"No, I'm from New Zealand. Auckland, to be exact. I met my husband there during the war." Her eyes momentarily darkened to deep jade, as if with remembered pain. "He's gone now, but I have my children. Jake, the oldest, and Patrick, who lives with his wife and children on the south end of our land. They've all kept me very busy."

"If you're ready, I'll take you back to town now." Jake's husky voice startled the two women, who had been deep in conversation.

"Oh, yes. I'm sorry if I took you away from any of your duties." Kelly stood up, successfully hiding her irritation at having to leave Maureen Cassidy so soon.

"I've enjoyed your visit, Kelly, even if it hasn't been planned," Maureen assured her. "How long will you be staying in this area?"

"I-I haven't decided," she suddenly stammered, refusing to look up at Jake, who was still standing nearby.

"I'd enjoy having you come again," the older woman told her. "Where are you staying?"

"At the hotel."

"The hotel!" Maureen looked horrified. "That's no place for a young woman alone to stay. It caters to cattle buyers who need some place to stay during their trips."

"I'm sure Miss James is quite used to being on her own." Jake's dry voice was mocking, which earned him a scathing look from Kelly.

"I'm fine there. You forget, I do quite a bit of traveling," Kelly replied, holding her hand out to Maureen. "Thank you."

"You really should stay for lunch," she protested.

"Miss James has to get back to town," Jake intervened.

Kelly wanted nothing more than to thwart this horrible man and accept Maureen's kind invitation, but she also wanted to get as far away from him as possible. "I really do have to be going," she said smoothly. "Thank you again."

The ride back to town was even more silent than the ride to Jake's house had been. When the Land-Rover stopped in front of the hotel,

Kelly didn't wait for Jake to come around to her side but scrambled down by herself.

"Kelly," he called after her.

She turned, throwing him a mutinous look. "What's wrong? Didn't I do a good enough job? Or are you afraid I said the wrong thing, after all?" she demanded. "I'm surprised you didn't stay there the entire time to make sure that I behaved myself."

"I just wanted to thank you for not saying anything to my mother," Jake said quietly. "We don't really get a lot of visitors out there, and I could tell that she enjoyed your talk together."

"It's nice that you're so respectful of your mother, Mr. Jake Cassidy," Kelly said heatedly. "Just as I am of my father's wishes. Because I didn't want to do this in the first place. I didn't want to come out here to this godforsaken land to deliver some sentimental message. But I came. I came because it was my father's last request. I haven't been the most obedient of daughters, so I thought that this was the least I could do for him. I'm just grateful he isn't here to see my failure." She spun around, walking into the hotel lobby without a backward glance.

Cal, who had been standing near the doorway, looked up at Jake with a broad grin on his face. "She's got somethin' of a temper, that one, Jake."

"That she has, Cal." Jake quickly shifted gears and drove off. "That she has," he muttered to himself.

Chapter Two

Still seething, Kelly went straight up to her room and quickly changed her clothes. Picking up a book, she flopped down on the bed and flipped to the page where she had left off. But she found herself unable to concentrate on the printed words in front of her. Jake Cassidy was too forceful a personality for her to shrug off.

Only the warning rumbles in her stomach drove Kelly downstairs for dinner. What had amazed her in the beginning was the large portions of food people were served. Leona, Cal's wife, was an excellent cook, and it took all of Kelly's willpower to refuse a dessert of apple pie served with clotted cream.

"But you're nothing but skin and bones!" Leona looked her over critically.

"Not really," Kelly replied. "I'm positive that I'll have to go on a diet when I get back home."

"I never thought we'd ever have anyone famous stay here."

"I'm not famous," Kelly protested. "The only reason I'm in so many magazines is because Pegasus advertises so heavily."

Leona looked down at her own ample girth with a smile. "I doubt I could ever get into those skinny jeans you young girls wear now. But Cal loves me the way I am, so I can't complain."

Kelly had seen the obvious love between the couple and wondered if she herself would ever find that kind of deep love between a man and a woman. So far the main ingredient had always been missing for her—the right man.

Kelly had already gotten used to the leisurely pace of small-town life and enjoyed the peace and quiet which were so different from the frantic pace she was used to keeping up. It was going to be difficult for her to return to New York.

That evening she stayed up late finishing her book and didn't get to sleep until past three o'clock. When, what seemed scant seconds later, the telephone by her bedside jangled noisily, she groaned sleepily and groped blindly for the phone.

"'Lo," she mumbled, her eyes still closed.

"Jake Cassidy here." His deep voice vibrated through Kelly's eardrums.

"Look, could you please call back later?" Kelly began to return the telephone receiver to the cradle. "Like at a decent hour."

"It's already six-thirty, and I've been up for quite some time. Besides, I'm calling at my mother's request."

Kelly sat up, pushing her heavy hair away from her face. She hated him for sounding wide awake and cheerful at this ungodly hour.

"It seems she doesn't feel right about your

35

staying at the hotel alone and wants you to come stay at the house." Jake sounded as if it were the last thing *he* wanted.

"Thank your mother for *her* kind invitation, but I'd prefer staying here," Kelly told him haughtily.

"I'll be in town at ten. Be ready then." The phone clicked in her ear.

"No, wait!" she called frantically into the now dead receiver. "Well, that's what he thinks," Kelly fumed, flopping back against the pillows and pulling the covers over her head. Tightly shutting her eyes, she was soon able to fall back asleep.

Kelly was lost in dreamland when her bed-covers were rudely pulled off her.

"What—!" Shocked and angry turquoise eyes met grim emerald ones as Kelly jumped to her feet.

"I told you to be ready at ten," Jake told her impatiently. "I don't have all day to wait around for you to decide to get out of bed."

"And *I* told *you* I was staying here," Kelly argued. "Besides, aren't you afraid I'll tell your mother my real reason for being here? Hey! What are you doing?" She watched in amazement as Jake picked up her suitcases and threw them on her bed. Then he opened the closet door, pulled her clothes from their hangers, and tossed them into the suitcases. After emptying the closet, he proceeded to empty the contents of the dresser drawers before going into the bathroom to dump Kelly's cosmetics into her tote bag.

"I suggest that you get dressed, unless you want to attract a lot of attention downstairs." Jake's eyes scornfully raked Kelly's light blue lace nightgown, which barely reached her thighs. "And don't worry about your supposed virtue. I'll wait downstairs. But not for long, so I suggest you get going, unless you want me to come back and dress you myself." The door slammed shut after his departing figure.

"Guess again, buster," Kelly muttered, dropping back onto the bed and sitting Indian style on the tumbled covers. It wouldn't take Jake very long to realize she wasn't going to follow along like some meek little lamb.

Then the wheels of her brain started clicking. Jake wouldn't be able to keep an eye on her twenty-four hours a day. He had a cattle station to run. Therefore, he'd be away from the house a great deal of the day. What better chance could she have for finding the right time to tell Maureen Cassidy her real reason for coming to Australia? Oh, yes, she'd outwit that insufferable man in the end.

With a satisfied smirk on her face, Kelly scrambled off the bed and quickly pulled on the pair of jeans and T-shirt that Jake had left her. She'd have to hurry, because she was sure Jake would enjoy coming back up here to dress her. He wasn't a man to make idle threats. With her suitcases already downstairs, Kelly had to stuff her nightgown into her purse and leave her face free of any makeup.

"Can't even put on clean clothes," she muttered, quickly brushing her hair and throwing her hairbrush back into her purse before leaving the room.

When Kelly reached the lobby, she could see Jake through the open front door; he was standing next to the Land-Rover, and her cases were already stowed inside.

"I understand you'll be staying with the Cassidys," Cal said heartily. "Sure gonna miss your pretty face around here. Nice of them to invite you, though."

"It seems the Cassidys can be a bit overpowering." Kelly's voice was tinged with sarcasm.

"They're real nice people." Obviously he had misunderstood the meaning of her words.

After Kelly paid her hotel bill, she walked outside, putting on her oversized sunglasses to block out the midmorning glare. Jake had the passenger door open for her, but he walked around to the driver's side without assisting her inside.

"I'm certainly glad you don't go to any trouble for li'l ol' me," she said caustically as she scrambled inside. "I hate it when people put on special manners just for my benefit."

"I'm sure you're so used to preferential treatment that this must be new for you." Jake's even voice irritated her even more.

"Oh, I can get used to just about anything, but I don't intend to get used to you. I believe that men should be much more civilized."

"Like that guy who's always photographed with you? Was he chosen to match you, or were you chosen to match him?" His voice held cold disdain.

"I guess you could say we're a matched pair," she joked.

"You probably live with him, too, I bet."

Kelly turned to look at Jake with surprise. Did he think that she and Kyle were lovers? Obviously he hadn't read any of the articles about their being twins. She immediately decided that she could have some fun with this.

"I guess you could say we do," she said carelessly. "You know the old saying: Two can live just as cheaply as one." Kelly was unprepared for the expression of cold disgust that Jake shot at her. She felt as if he had struck her.

"My mother has much higher moral standards than you seem to have, so I suggest that you don't let her know what a little tramp you are."

Kelly clenched her fists, seething in anger. "Don't worry; I've learned to act the part of a lady quite well," she said coldly. "I wouldn't dream of disgracing your family, and your mother in particular." She sat back in her seat, refusing to look or speak to him for the remainder of the drive to the station.

When the Land-Rover pulled up in front of the house, Maureen was on the porch to greet her guest.

"I'm so glad you decided to accept my invitation," the older woman said warmly. "That hotel is not meant for young women traveling alone."

"I'm sure Miss James could have handled herself." Jake's sarcastic comment earned him a glance of reproof from his mother.

"Lunch will be ready in fifteen minutes, if you'd like to freshen up first," Maureen told Kelly before turning to Jake. "I'm giving her the middle guest room."

Jake merely nodded as he pulled the suitcases out of the back of the Land-Rover and carried them inside, leaving Kelly and Maureen to follow.

"I have to check on lunch," Maureen said as she turned to Kelly, "so why don't you follow Jake down to your room?"

The last thing Kelly wanted was to be alone with Jake again, but she couldn't think of a plausible excuse not to do as Maureen had suggested. She followed Jake's broad back down a hall and through an open door to the left.

Kelly fell in love with the room at first glance. The walls were painted a pale green, with one wall papered in a coordinated, muted print. Green-and-blue shag carpeting was soft and plushy underfoot. The light-colored furniture and pale blue bedspread completed the light and airy atmosphere. Opened doors led out to a vine-covered veranda.

"Disappointed?" Jake's sarcastic voice intruded on her silent admiration of the room. "A real mattress instead of a rope bed. Electricity, hot and cold running water, even indoor plumbing."

"How convenient." She matched his tone.

40

"Thank you so much for carrying my bags in."

Recognizing the curt dismissal in her voice, Jake grinned, tipping an imaginary hat as he sketched a mocking bow.

"Yes, ma'am; thank you, ma'am."

"Oh, get out!" Kelly shouted, unable to stand any more of his gibes.

"The dining room is at the other end of the house, in the back," Jake told her as he walked out of the room, closing the door behind him.

Kelly took her anger out on her suitcases, lugging the heaviest one over to the bed and opening it. After muttering over the crumpled condition of her clothes, thanks to Jake, she quickly hung them up.

She washed quickly in the blue- and silver-appointed bathroom, then applied a light application of makeup, brushed her hair, and changed into a pair of black cord jeans and a jade silk shirt.

Feeling more like herself, she left her room, following the directions Jake had given her to the dining room. Maureen was already there, placing a large tureen on the table. She smiled on seeing Kelly standing in the doorway.

"We don't stand on ceremony here." Maureen waved toward one of the chairs. "Jake usually eats the midday meal with the men, but, as they've already eaten, he'll eat with us today. In fact, he should have been back here by now. He had to go out to speak to one of the men."

"A place this large must be quite a responsibility," Kelly commented, trying to hide the dismay she felt at knowing that Jake would be present at the meal. She had hoped he would be too eager to get back to his work to eat with them.

"Jake has been running the station since he was seventeen," Maureen replied.

"Seventeen?" Kelly's face wore a puzzled frown. "But I thought your husband died just five years ago."

"John had been an invalid for many years." The older woman's eyes reflected remembered pain. "While helping with breaking the horses one year, he was thrown off and broke his back."

Kelly uttered a horrified gasp. He must have been in his prime, close to the age Jake Cassidy was now. The thought of him—or of Jake!—confined to a wheelchair was frightening. "That must have been hard on you," she murmured.

"The one who truly suffered was Jake." Maureen sighed. "He was too young to have to take on such a difficult task. There were a lot of heated arguments here when it was time for Jake to go to the university." She smiled. "John's accident didn't impair his voice. Those two turned the air blue with their words. But Jake went to the university and graduated with honors."

Kelly was not surprised to hear that he had done so well at school, although she would have thought he was not the sort to worry about higher education at all.

"What my mother means is that I can count without using my fingers and toes." Jake's mocking voice came from the doorway behind Kelly.

"Oh, you mean you carry around a pocket calculator?" Kelly asked sweetly.

Jake's eyes narrowed to emerald slits. "You've got a sharp tongue on you, Kelly James."

"Jake, stop picking on the poor girl," Maureen scolded her son. "I suggest we sit down and eat before the stew gets cold. Show Kelly that even out here we do have manners."

Kelly caught the gleam in the emerald eyes and recognized the challenge he was throwing her way. She wouldn't refuse it, either.

Lunch consisted of a filling and tasty lamb stew. Kelly was aware of Jake's eyes on her during the meal, but she easily evaded his gaze.

"Do you happen to ride horses?" Jake asked, forcing Kelly to look at him.

"Yes, I do," she replied, but both of them let the matter drop there.

"How ever did you get started in modeling?" Maureen asked, unaware of the undercurrent of tension between her son and her guest.

"My mother enrolled me in a modeling course when I was in high school. She wanted her gawky teenager to learn a few social graces," she explained. "My brother also attended. Just for the fun of it, at first, but he quickly learned that he enjoyed standing around being admired by pretty girls. It was difficult for me to adjust to being taller than most of the boys my age, so modeling was an outlet for me then, but it turned into a career. It's hard work, but I love it."

"The glamour, the bright lights, meeting famous people," Jake murmured, mockery lacing his voice. "It's tough."

A little while later, Maureen excused herself and left the room.

"Look, it's only too obvious that you don't like me," Kelly told Jake once they were alone. "And that doesn't bother me one bit, except that you invited me here and—"

"Correction: My mother invited you."

"All right, your mother invited me. So I'll make a deal with you for the duration of my visit. I won't tell your mother about my father as long as you're civil to me." Her voice was crisp and businesslike. "Do you think you can handle something that simple?"

Jake leaned back in his chair, viewing her with admiration. "Do I have to sign it in blood, or will a verbal agreement be acceptable?"

"I'm sure you can be trusted," Kelly told him coolly. "After all, this is more beneficial to you than it is to me. I'm only trying to carry out my father's last request," she finished sarcastically.

When Maureen returned to the dining room with dessert, Kelly had a pleasant smile on her face but Jake was looking grim.

"None for me." Jake uncoiled himself from his chair. "I have a lot of work to catch up on. I'm sure you two can find enough to amuse you this afternoon." He shot Kelly an amused glance, and she raised her glass in a mocking salute.

After their meal, Maureen took Kelly on a tour of the house. The younger woman was amazed by the size and modernity of everything she saw, not to mention the fact that each room was tastefully decorated in a different color scheme.

"Jake makes sure we have every comfort out here," Maureen told her, gesturing toward the large entertainment center in the den. "I usually travel to Sydney two or three times a year to shop for clothes and any items that I can't buy in town."

"Isn't it lonely out here for you sometimes?"

"You don't have time to be lonely when you have household help to supervise and a garden that needs constant attention. The wife of one of our stockmen comes in to help with the housework, and another one does the cooking. Myrna, our cook, thinks of herself as a tyrant in the true sense of the word. She's in town visiting her daughter this afternoon." Maureen smiled. "She and her husband have been here longer than I have."

"You mentioned that you grew up in New Zealand," Kelly said casually. "Is it very different here?"

"Very. In fact, in the beginning I hated it here. I was a city girl. To me, beef was something you saw served on a plate, not walking around."

Kelly had to smile at the apt description. That was the way she had always pictured beef, too.

"I shouldn't speak of the past." Maureen's voice grew brisk. "Come on; I'll show you my garden."

Outside in the warm summer sunshine, Maureen showed Kelly an Olympic-sized swimming pool and a colorful flower-filled garden.

"This is my therapy, actually," Maureen explained, leaning over to inhale a fragrant blossom. "I was determined to have color all around me. In that I've succeeded. And I wasn't very well a while back, either, but my garden kept me outside and helped me to recover."

During the course of the afternoon Kelly discovered more about the older woman and the life she led on the large cattle station. They sat in easy chairs on the shady porch, drinking iced tea and relaxing. Kelly's eyes occasionally strayed toward the large barns and the corrals filled with horses to catch a glimpse of a tall, commanding figure in mud-colored cords and tan open-necked shirt.

"We don't dress for dinner here," Maureen told her later as she noticed the hour.

"Well, I would like to take a shower first," Kelly replied; she was not yet used to the hot, sticky weather. "I still haven't gotten acclimatized."

"Yes, it does take some getting used to. Dinner won't be ready for about an hour, so you have plenty of time."

Since she had the extra time, Kelly opted for a hot bubble bath. Soaking in the delicately scented water, she mused over the events of the past few days. A smile curved her lips as she recalled the high-handed way Jake had taken over her life, something Kelly had never allowed any man to do. She had always been determined that no man would rule her.

"If Kyle could see me now," she said aloud to herself, looking amused. "He'd laugh himself silly and want to know Jake Cassidy's secret."

After her bath, Kelly wrapped herself up in a towel and looked into the mirror to apply her makeup. She used a blue eye shadow and skillfully blended a rose-colored shade with it to deepen her turquoise eyes. After dusting blusher across her cheekbones, she brushed her hair, leaving it loose and pinning the sides back with combs.

She dressed in deep teal pants and a matching gauze tunic top edged with gold. She slipped a gold twist belt around her waist and applied perfume. Then she left her room, heading for the other end of the house.

Jake was there ahead of her, holding a glass of whiskey in one hand. His black hair gleamed from a recent shower. Kelly couldn't help but notice how his cream-colored slacks clung to his lean hips and his navy silk shirt couldn't disguise his broad shoulders. As if sensing her presence, he turned, raising his glass in a salute.

"What will you have?" he asked her.

"White wine, please."

"I suppose my mother has taken you on the

grand tour." Jake handed her a filled wine-glass.

"Yes. You have a beautiful house," Kelly replied. "I can see why you're so proud of it."

"This must seem pretty primitive compared to a penthouse apartment," he said sarcastically. "I assume that's what you and your boyfriend live in."

"Not exactly." She refused to rise to his bait. "I believe in the simple life."

Jake picked up a magazine and tossed it, open, onto a table. Kelly instantly recognized the pictures of a fashion layout she and Kyle had done in New Orleans during Mardi Gras the previous year. She secretly wondered how Jake could miss seeing the strong resemblance between her and Kyle, especially after she had mentioned that her brother had gone to modeling school. She thought of setting him straight here and now, but an imp of mischief prompted her to continue the charade.

One photo showed her in a white lacy handkerchief dress, with Kyle in black pants and a white silk shirt in contrast. Kelly's long hair was pulled back with dark blue ribbons threaded through the tousled curls. Seated on a white-painted wrought-iron garden bench, she looked up at Kyle's face with a dreamy expression. She was the picture of provocative innocence.

"The simple life?" Jake asked dryly. "Sure."

Kelly took a deep breath, trying to control her anger as she silently counted to ten. She had never known a man who could cause her to lose her temper as easily as this insufferable man could. "I do believe we made a pact," she finally said in an acid-sweet voice.

"What pact?" Maureen entered the room, smiling at the two of them.

"Kelly's agreed not to molest me during the day so I can get my work done if I keep my bedroom door unlocked at night," Jake said blandly.

To her mortification, Kelly could feel her cheeks burning in embarrassment. The glitter in Jake's eyes told her he was aware of her distress and was enjoying it.

"Jake!" his mother reproved. "That isn't a very nice thing to say. In fact, you've shocked the poor girl."

"She'll survive," he replied dryly. "Do you want a drink?"

"No. Myrna said we're to go in now or she'll refuse to feed us."

Jake smoothly interposed himself between the two women as he escorted them into the large dining room.

That evening Kelly was able to meet Myrna. A small, vigorous woman in her late sixties, she seemed to radiate the energy of a woman half her age. Her keen eyes noted every inch of Kelly with alarming thoroughness.

"So you travel all over the world to wear these crazy new fashions and have your picture taken." Her speech was brisker than the usual Australian drawl that Kelly was becoming accustomed to hearing. "Don't you ever eat?"

"Once a week," she replied evenly.

Myrna's eyes showed admiration. "At least she's got spirit without acting high-notioned," she told Maureen. "Not like some we know who live around here."

"That will be all, Myrna." Jake's voice cracked like a whip through the air.

"Some people forget that I used to change their diapers for them." Myrna was undaunted as she walked back into the kitchen.

Kelly hid a smile; she had enjoyed seeing Jake taken down a peg.

"You must excuse Myrna," Maureen apologized. "She believes in speaking her mind. Myrna and Jake have their spats several times a day. It's something you become used to around here."

Kelly felt surprised by Maureen's assumption that she would be there long enough to become accustomed to anything. At that moment, twenty-four hours in Jake's company was twenty-four hours too long! She bent her head to concentrate on her roast beef.

After dinner Maureen and Kelly enjoyed a quiet evening listening to records in the den. Although her pose was relaxed, Kelly's every nerve was aware of Jake's hooded gaze, which remained focused on her profile.

"I think I'll go to bed." Kelly finally rose, desperate to break the spell cast by Jake's unnerving gaze. "Good night."

"Good night, Kelly." Maureen smiled, while Jake merely nodded uninterestedly as if he couldn't care less what she did.

Safely inside her room, Kelly closed the doors that opened onto the veranda. It didn't take her long to clean her face of makeup and change into dark pink cotton shortie pajamas. She curled up in bed with a pad on her drawn-up knees to begin a letter to Kyle. A smile flitted across her face as her pen flew across the paper. An hour later she put the pad aside and slid down between the covers, switching the light off. She soon fell into a deep sleep.

Kelly was up early the next morning, feeling refreshed after her sound sleep. After a quick shower she brushed her hair, leaving it loose about her face. After she had dressed in jeans and a multicolored plaid cotton shirt, she headed for the dining room.

Maureen was seated at the table, drinking coffee and reading a newspaper. She looked up with a welcoming smile when Kelly entered.

"After being used to looking out and seeing snow and more snow, I enjoy seeing all this sunshine," Kelly told her as she poured herself a cup of coffee and sat down.

Myrna stuck her head out of the kitchen and called to Kelly, "I'll have your breakfast ready in a few minutes."

"Oh, I don't eat breakfast. Just coffee is fine for me," Kelly replied.

"That's what you think," the cook said tartly. "You'll eat what I fix you." The door swung shut after her.

Maureen chuckled. "As I said, no one can

get the best of Myrna. She's convinced she knows what's best for everyone. My advice is to eat what you can."

Since she was not used to eating first thing in the morning, Kelly was surprised to find she was able to do justice to the eggs, sausage, and toast Myrna set before her.

"Jake is going to show you the barns after lunch," Maureen commented. "He ate breakfast hours ago and he'll have lunch with the men, but he'll come back up here for you afterwards."

Kelly silently wondered whose idea that had been, and she quickly came to the conclusion that it must have been Maureen's suggestion. Jake wouldn't volunteer to escort her anywhere, even if his life depended on it, she was sure.

Kelly spent a quiet morning with Maureen; then, after lunch, she walked out onto the porch and looked toward the large barns and surrounding corrals. Even from a distance it was not hard to recognize the tall, dark-haired figure standing with a group of men. A few moments later the tall figure separated itself from the group and walked with long, unhurried strides toward the house.

Kelly stood at the top of the steps, leaning against a post. Jake stopped below her, resting one booted foot on the bottom step and flashing her a mocking grin. She felt at a disadvantage and realized that she was more uncomfortable about this tour than he was. If anything, he looked prepared to enjoy every minute of it—at her expense.

Even in dust-covered tan cords, a sweat-stained shirt, and a dark brown hat, Jake was a virile and good-looking man. A man used to being in charge, giving orders. And to having his way with the opposite sex.

"Come on," Jake said indifferently, as if he couldn't care less whether she accompanied him or not.

"I hate the thought of taking you away from your work," Kelly said sweetly as she walked down the steps. "Perhaps someone else could show me around and let you get back to whatever you were doing."

"I'll show you around myself," he said grimly.

Most of the stockmen, Kelly was told, were out rounding up the new calves for branding. The few men near the barns viewed the tall, honey-blond young woman with more than casual interest as she and their boss passed them. One gray-haired man watched from the open doorway of one of the barns. "She sure can't be a new jillaroo, Jake," he called out with a wide grin on his face.

Noticing Kelly's confused frown, Jake explained. "A jillaroo is what we call a young woman who works on a station. She usually cooks for the men, and so on. A jackaroo is a student stockman, so to speak." He raised his voice. "Will, this is Kelly James. She's visiting Mother for a while." He turned back to Kelly. "Will is Myrna's husband; he's in charge of the cattle barns. We couldn't do without him on this half of the station." When Kelly looked questioningly at him, he explained further.

"Besides running cattle, I also run merino sheep south of here. My brother is in charge of that area."

Will's brown eyes snapped with life as he stepped forward. "My wife said you're a pretty thing with lots of spirit. Course, not too many people like to swap words with Myrna. They always lose." He chuckled.

Kelly smiled, instantly drawn to the sprightly older man. But Jake's hand was already at the small of her back, steering her toward the interior of the barns, and she had no time to say anything to Will.

"Watch your step," Jake warned with an amused smile.

She glared at him, retorting, "I do that every time I'm around you."

Will slapped his thigh and chortled as he walked away. "Yes, sir, looks like Myrna could be right."

Kelly silently questioned the old man's statement as she looked around, letting her eyes adjust to the dim interior. Her nose twitched at the pungent scents of warm horseflesh, oiled leather and hay. As she walked down the length of the barn, Jake named each horse for her. Unable to resist the heads hanging over the stall doors, Kelly stopped to pat each one in turn, crooning softly to them.

"You *do* know something about horses," Jake commented in surprise.

"My older brother breeds and races quarter horses," she said briefly.

Kelly was amazed as they left the horses behind and Jake led her through a large milking barn, a small dairy, and the various sheds that housed the machinery necessary to maintain the large station. She was very conscious of the curious stares she received as they went back outside and walked over the land. Any introductions Jake made were curt and almost rude.

"What's that building for over there?" she asked, pointing toward a large, barnlike shed away from the other buildings.

"That's where we freeze the slaughtered beef," Jake replied. "Because of the long distances in this country, it's better if each rancher slaughters and freezes his own beef and flies it out to market. I didn't think you'd care to see the interior."

Kelly shuddered, her mind's eye showing her a very gruesome picture. "No, I wouldn't." Jake steered her back toward the house; he was apparently quite eager to get rid of her. "I apologize again for taking you away from your work," she said. "I realize that your mother probably insisted you do this, not knowing how much you would detest showing me around."

Jake said nothing, merely smiled. His eyes were focused on a pale green car which was stopping beside the house. Kelly's eyes followed his gaze, and she saw the driver get out and wave in their direction.

"Jake! Jake, darling!" A feminine voice carried across the yard.

Kelly raised an eyebrow as she turned to look at the tall man beside her. "Jake, darling?" she murmured.

The woman walked toward them, the warm smile on her face clearly meant for Jake. Her burnished auburn hair shone brightly in the afternoon sun, and her olive-green pantsuit set off her fair coloring and petite figure.

"I came by to make sure you hadn't forgotten about this evening." Her eyes flickered curiously over Kelly, then slid away uninterestedly.

"I hadn't forgotten," Jake told her. "Sheila, this is Kelly James. Kelly, Sheila Lonnigan. Sheila's father owns the station closest to ours." He turned to Sheila. "Kelly is visiting my mother for a few weeks."

"Oh." The other woman relaxed visibly. "Well, I do hope you enjoy your visit, Miss James. Are you an American?"

"Yes, I am." Kelly was silently curious about the relationship between the tall, black-haired man and the lovely auburn-haired woman, and she berated herself for her interest.

Sheila rested her hand on Jake's arm, smiling up at him in an intimate fashion. "Seven?" she murmured, as if they were alone.

"I'll be there." He returned her smile warmly.

"Perhaps Maureen will bring you to our house for tea one day, Miss James." Sheila left her hand on Jake's arm as she spoke, a clearly possessive gesture meaning hands off.

"That would be nice. Thank you." Kelly's words were polite, although she didn't mean a single one of them.

"I'll see you at seven." Sheila returned her attention to Jake. "Goodbye, Miss James." She turned and walked with easy grace back to her car.

Kelly and Jake watched the car leave in silence. "She hates me," Kelly said offhandedly.

Jake looked at her in surprise. "Isn't that a little strong, considering you've only just met? Besides, Sheila is a warm and loving woman."

To you, I'm sure she's that and more, Kelly thought cattily to herself. "Think what you like. My intuition hasn't been wrong yet. Of course, it isn't her fault she isn't tall and willowy. Now, if you'll excuse me, I'd like to take a long, leisurely bath and wash my hair before dinner."

"Kelly." Jake's voice followed her as she walked toward the house. "A horse will be at your disposal during your stay here. All I request is that you don't ride alone."

Without slowing a step, she nodded to show that she had heard his words.

Chapter Three

As the days passed, Kelly continued to enjoy the relaxed pace of the sprawling cattle station. Several times she had gone horseback riding with Will as a companion. Jake himself was gone many evenings, dining with Sheila Lonnigan, Kelly surmised. It never occurred to her that he might be the reason she lay awake those nights until she heard the muted sounds of the front door opening and his heavy tread in the hallway. Only then would she finally fall asleep.

Late one afternoon Kelly lazed on a terry-cloth-covered lounge chair; Maureen had settled herself in a nearby chair under a large umbrella. She had refused to go swimming with Kelly, whose slender form was clad in only a brief black bikini which accented her golden tan.

"I must speak to Jake about having a party," Maureen commented. "This must be so boring for you, and it would give you a chance to meet some of the people who live around here. We pride ourselves on our parties, even if I do say so myself."

"Oh, no," Kelly protested, propping herself

up on her elbows. "It's been wonderful not having to worry about how I look and not to be rushing around all the time. Although I'm definitely going to have to go on a diet when I return to New York. I'm turning into a regular butterball." Kelly looked bemusedly down at herself. When she looked back up, she was disconcerted to find Jake's green eyes on her. He stared at her tanned legs, then slowly moved his gaze upward over her exposed flesh, lingering at her slightly parted lips before meeting her eyes. Kelly felt as if it were his hands instead of his eyes moving with such familiarity over her body. The thought caused her blood to race madly through her veins.

Jake finally broke the spell as he took a pack of cigarettes out of his shirt pocket and slowly lit one. Kelly couldn't keep her eyes from this rawly virile man. Jake's black boots were caked with mud, as were the legs of his jeans. His denim shirt stuck to his broad chest in damp patches. His jaw was shadowed with the beginnings of a beard, adding to the rough male picture he presented. He was a man who belonged to the outdoors. No woman would ever be able to wrap him around her finger. He would always be his own man—possessive and demanding, even as a lover. Kelly tingled at the thought of Jake in the role of lover. That he would be excellent she had no doubts.

"Why don't you take a swim?" Maureen suggested, unaware of the crosscurrents of tension flowing between her son and her guest. "Are you staying in for dinner this evening, Jake? We haven't seen too much of you lately."

Jake nodded, replying, "I already told Myrna I'd be here." His eyes flickered over Kelly in a hooded gaze. "A swim sounds good."

After he disappeared into the house, Maureen returned to her book. "Sheila's been running after Jake for years now," she told Kelly. "Oh, there was a time when she gave up and married a land broker in Sydney. But she divorced him two years ago, took back her maiden name, and came back here to stay with her father and mother, taking up where she left off with Jake." Maureen's voice sounded disapproving.

Kelly grinned, sensing that the older woman didn't care for the fiery Sheila. "My father always used to say that women with red hair have tempers to match. They have the kind of fire a man can't always handle, and he tends to get burned."

Maureen's face paled for a moment; then she grew pensive. "Do you resemble your father, Kelly?"

"No, I mostly take after my mother, although my older brother, Michael, looks very much like him."

Maureen put down her book as if to say more, but she was interrupted by Jake's arrival. Kelly's eyes widened slightly as she took in the muscular bronze chest matted with crisp black hair. Jake's brief black trunks hugged his lean hips like a second skin. Kelly could feel strange stirrings within her body as she watched Jake make a clean dive into the sun-warmed water and swim with sure strokes over to the side of the pool. He shook his wet hair out of his eyes and aimed them at Kelly.

"Coming in?" he asked with a grin on his face.

"Why not?" Kelly rose, stretching her limbs with the sinuous grace of a cat, purposely looking away from the burning eyes that were trained on her. She bent over, brushing her hair into a ponytail on top of her head and securing it with an elastic band. She padded over to the side of the pool a short distance from Jake and dove in.

Kelly surfaced, enjoying the feel of the cool water against her heated skin. She purposely kept away from Jake, who seemed content to swim the length of the pool several times with easy strokes.

"So those two sexy scraps of cloth aren't just for show, after all." Jake's voice startled her out of her musings. "Even if you do float more than you swim."

Kelly was glad she was near the side of the pool and was able to grab the cement edge. "Years ago, when they accused someone of being a witch they'd throw her into a pond. If she sank to the bottom, that meant she wasn't a witch. But if she floated . . ." Kelly deliberately paused, her deep turquoise eyes sparkling brightly.

Jake gripped the pool edge on either side of Kelly; she couldn't escape if she wanted to. She was uncomfortably aware of his bare chest just grazing her breasts as their bodies floated against each other in the buoyant water. Jake's green eyes glittered with the hard brilliance of emeralds.

"Ah, and a witch you are, Kelly James," Jake taunted softly. "Not the kind of witch you pretend to be, but a much more dangerous kind."

Kelly's breath caught in her throat at Jake's rough velvet voice.

"The most dangerous and the best kind," he concluded, before swimming away from her without bothering to explain his words.

Kelly looked around, grateful that Maureen had disappeared into the house. Unwilling to stay near Jake any longer, she hauled herself out of the pool, grabbed her terry-cloth cover-up, and beat a hasty retreat to the house. She felt even more mortified when she heard Jake's low laugh following her escape.

Kelly took a long shower, letting the sting-ing spray relax her tense muscles while she washed the chlorine from her hair. Then, with a dangerous gleam in her eye, she dressed for dinner in bright rose-pink silk pants and a matching tunic top, unbuttoning the front low enough to display a fair amount of cleavage. After setting her hair on hot rollers, she brushed the silky curls into place, pulling one side back and securing the hair with a bright pink comb to let the curls tum-ble down her back. By the time she finished putting on her makeup and dabbing on her perfume she felt ready to face anything—or anyone.

Jake's hooded eyes revealed nothing as he took in Kelly's deliberately seductive outfit a few minutes later. Dressed in black pants and a black silk shirt, he was himself the picture of dangerous attraction, and Kelly vowed to beware. With some alarm, Kelly turned from Jake to notice Maureen's wan features and asked the older woman if she felt unwell.

"I just feel a little tired," Maureen admitted. "I'm sure that dinner will make me feel better."

The meal was delicious, though Kelly really couldn't eat much. The dual distractions of Jake's sharp gaze and Maureen's ill health had her too much on edge to enjoy her food.

Once dessert was over, Jake suggested to his mother that she go to her room. She admitted that she was still tired and turned to Kelly, an apology in her voice as she excused herself and hoped that Kelly would be all right for the evening.

Kelly assured her that she would be fine and urged Maureen to get her rest. After the older woman left to go to her room, Jake rose from the table, murmuring that he had paperwork to do.

I didn't realize my company was that bad, Kelly thought to herself, feeling her irritation rise.

Later, sitting alone in the den listening to records, she could feel her anger mounting further still. On impulse, she picked up an empty coffee cup and filled it from the small pot. Then she walked down to the closed door that Maureen had once pointed out as Jake's office and knocked briskly. She opened the door after a gruff voice bade her enter.

"I brought you some coffee," she said inanely, holding up the cup.

"Thanks, but I have some." Jake nodded toward an insulated flask on his desk.

"Oh." Kelly suddenly felt foolish.

"I would have thought you could come up with a more imaginative excuse than that." His eyes openly mocked her.

"Excuse?"

"To come in here. After all, we're virtually alone now that my mother's gone to bed."

Kelly set the cup down on top of a nearby bookcase before she gave in to her impulse to throw the contents in Jake's face. "You're the last man I'd care to be alone with," Kelly snapped. "When I make a play for a man, I choose one who's a gentleman, not nine-tenths machine. You're nothing more than a computer that receives the necessary data and digests it for future use. Emotions mean nothing to you; that's why you won't let me tell your mother who I am. No wonder everyone thinks the great Jake Cassidy is infallible; he has a computer terminal for a heart!" she lashed out as she turned away, eager only to leave the room. Her hand had barely brushed the doorknob when she was roughly spun around and pressed against the door by Jake's hard body.

"A computer terminal, is it?" Jake growled. "Let's see how much of me is made of machinery, shall we?"

Kelly was unable to struggle as his mouth

descended on hers in a punishing kiss. Her senses whirled in a kaleidoscope of reactions as Jake forced her mouth open to explore further. She was vaguely aware of the door panels pressing into her back, and she was certain that they would leave an imprint on her skin forever as a memory of this.

"You *are* a witch," Jake muttered thickly against her lips as his fingers twisted cruelly in her hair, forcing her to look up at him. "How many men have kissed you this way? Have held you in their arms like this before they dumped you into their beds?"

Kelly tried to protest that no other man had ever kissed her with such force, but the words refused to come out.

"Damn it, I don't care." Jake's rough voice sounded as if he were angrier with himself than with her as he recaptured her lips for another mind-shattering kiss. Under his touch, the flames leaped up in Kelly's body. Her arms crept up to encircle Jake's neck; her fingers tangled in his thick, shaggy hair as he pressed her body closer to his as if to absorb it.

Jake's hands pulled her shirt above the waistband of her pants, moving caressingly along the sensitive skin of her spine. Kelly was boneless under his touch, clay to be molded to his specifications. She uttered a soft sigh of protest when his lips left hers to move along her jawline to her ear, pulling the lobe with his teeth. They slowly moved back toward her mouth, taking their time. Unable to stand the torture of waiting, Kelly turned her face to seek his lips. She wanted them against hers again in that hard, demanding kiss. She was dejected when the pressure of Jake's mouth softened.

"We have company," he murmured against her lips.

It was a few seconds before Kelly's dazed senses could realize that someone was knocking at the door.

"Jake? You in there?" Liam, Jake's head stockman, could be heard through the thick panels of the door as he tried the handle without success. Obviously Jake had locked the door without her noticing. "You said you wanted that list of stock to be shipped out by tonight."

"Right." Kelly was surprised to hear Jake's voice sounding so controlled after the passion he had just displayed. One hand pressed her hot cheek against his chest while his arms still held her trembling form against him. "Do me a favor and go out to the kitchen and ask Myrna for more coffee first, and bring a cup for yourself."

Jake released Kelly, looking down at her flushed face as he pushed her hair back, his hand lingering on the silky strands.

"It's a good thing Liam interrupted us when he did," he commented. "Otherwise, we'd be making very good use of the couch over there."

Jake's words acted like a whip on Kelly's raw nerves. Desiring only to hurt him back, she struck out wildly, her hand making sharp contact with his cheek. Then she spun around, fumbling with the lock, but her shoulders were roughly grasped before she could make her escape. Pulling the door open, Kelly shook Jake's hands free.

"Don't you ever touch me again!" she spat before running blindly to her room, ignoring Jake's commands for her to return.

Once she reached the safety of her room, Kelly leaned back against the door, pressing her hands against her heated cheeks. She couldn't understand it! It wasn't as if she hadn't been kissed before. Kelly had done more than her share of fending off overly amorous admirers. But with Jake her defenses hadn't been enough to stop him in time and she had been very thoroughly kissed, awakening senses she hadn't known existed. For him it had only been a reaction to her taunts about his masculinity, but to her it had been much more. Kelly wondered bitterly if Jake had any emotions at all. A man could feel physical desire for a woman without feeling any emotion, and Kelly was sure that Jake was a man like that.

She hurriedly undressed and washed her face, unable to miss seeing the slight glaze still in her eyes. Switching off the light, she agitatedly paced the room, wrapping her arms around her body as if she were cold, although the night air was very warm. And every time she thought of Jake's kiss, heat rose in her body. It was almost dawn before she finally flopped into bed and fell into a fitful sleep.

Kelly rose at her normal time, feeling even more uptight than she had when she went to bed. Deciding to go for a ride after breakfast, she donned well-worn jeans and a pale green blouse. Since she didn't want to hear any comments on the dark circles under her eyes, she applied a cover-up cream to hide the ravages of her restless night.

At breakfast, Kelly was told that Maureen would be resting in bed for the day.

"Is she very ill?" Kelly asked, remembering how tired the older woman had looked the previous evening.

"No, her heart just took a big strain when she was sick last winter and she needs her rest more than she thinks she does," Myrna replied. "If Jake wasn't such a fool, he'd get married and let his wife take the load of this house from her shoulders."

Kelly silently thought that Sheila Lonnigan would be only too happy to do just that. "Perhaps he will," she murmured, idly stirring her coffee.

"Well, if it's that viper-tongued redhead, you can be sure *I* won't be around to take orders from her," Myrna said tartly, walking back into the kitchen.

Kelly smiled at the cook's words as she lifted her coffee cup to her lips. Then her smile disappeared as she thought of Maureen. Even though she had promised Jake to keep silent about her real reasons for being there, she still felt very strongly about telling Maureen the truth. All she had to do was find the right time and the right way.

After breakfast, her wide-brimmed hat in one hand, Kelly walked out to the barns. Will halted in the doorway, flashing her a good-morning grin.

"Looks like you're looking to go riding," he called out.

"Only if I can kidnap you to go with me," Kelly cheerfully replied. From the beginning, she had made it clear to the older man that she did not want to take him away from his duties and he was to tell her if she wanted to go riding at an inconvenient time. But she had an idea that Will would never let her know if her timing was bad.

Their back-and-forth bantering had already become a habit, developed when Kelly spent time at the barns. From the first, she had insisted on saddling and unsaddling the mare she usually rode, as well as walking her until she was cooled out and grooming her. It was during her rides and her visits to the barn that Kelly had learned more about the station and, especially, the man in charge of it. Will also enjoyed telling her the history of Australia's early days, when it had been as untamed and wild as the American West.

"You ain't the only ones to boast about a big gold strike in those days," he had told her in his gravelly voice. "We had a big gold strike here in 1851. An E. H. Hargreaves had returned from the goldfields in California and discovered gold here in New South Wales. There's even some towns that still resemble the boom towns of those years."

"And what about Ned Kelly?" Kelly had prompted him. "I've heard about him. That he was a bushranger."

"Bushranger, killer, bandit. They're all the same," Will had told her. "To many he's a national hero. He was quite a one for the ladies. They just couldn't seem to resist him. He was a man who really stood for himself."

Just like Jake, Kelly had thought to herself.

"There are pictures of him in his homemade suit of armor. That's really something to see." Will warmed to his favorite subject, the history of Australia. "You can see his armor on display at the Melbourne museum. He had courage and the guts to prove it where many only talked about it. He even talked back to the judge who handed down his death sentence. He was hanged in November 1880. So you can't talk just about your Jesse James and the shootout at the O.K. Corral. We have our share, too."

"It sounds like a life Jake would have fit into quite nicely," Kelly had commented idly. "Deep down, I'm sure he has the makings of a good bushranger."

"Jake seems a bit rough, but he has a bigger heart than most of us put together. When we had our bad years, Jake put us before himself. Old John Cassidy used to say that if his men did a good job for him, he would do everything in his power to take care of them. And Jake's a good man, like his father before him. It was hard for him to take up where Old John left off, especially being so young at the time. But he dug right in with the rest of us and didn't take on no airs. Course, he still had a lot to learn." Will had chuckled. "There were some of us who gave him a rough time, but he always took it like his father did. He never asks anything of his men that he wouldn't do himself, whether it comes to breaking horses or just fixing fences. He's always out there doing more than his share."

Kelly thought over that conversation as she saddled up the bay mare she rode, Lady Anne.

"Let me put this tack away and I'll get my horse saddled in a jiffy," Will told her as he held up a bridle he had been repairing.

"I'll accompany the lady this morning, Will."

Kelly whirled around to face Jake, but she was unable to read anything in his expression. One hand grasped the reins of the huge black stallion he always rode. Unwittingly, she thought how appropriate that was—a devil's horse for a devil.

"Perhaps I would prefer Will's company," she said huskily.

"And *I* prefer that Will stay here and continue with his duties," Jake said grimly.

"Of course, I forgot. You're the boss. What you say goes," Kelly said coldly.

"That's right."

Kelly knew that she couldn't suddenly refuse to go without making a scene, although she would almost prefer that to being alone with Jake again. Knowing better than to try, though, she silently fumed instead. Jake looped his horse's reins over a post and stepped forward to assist Kelly in mounting. With blazing eyes, she jerked her arm away and nimbly pulled herself into the saddle. Jake's jaw merely hardened as he retrieved his mount's reins and mounted himself. As they rode off they didn't hear Will's gleeful chuckle as he watched them leave.

With Jake's horse in the lead, Kelly was forced to follow him along the cattle trails. She pulled her hatbrim down to shade her eyes from the bright sun, leaning slightly forward in the saddle as Jake nudged his horse into a canter and her horse quickly followed suit. The cattle grazing in the lush pastures moved slowly out of the way of the two swift horses. As they were traveling in a direction Kelly was not familiar with, she had no choice but to go on following the large black stallion and his rider. She had no idea where they were, or how far from the house. By the time Jake slowed his horse, Kelly's shirt was sticking to her back in wet patches. Jake turned in the saddle, waiting for her to catch up with him.

"Isn't this a little fast for the horses in this heat?" she asked sulkily.

"Why didn't you come back when I called you last night?" Jake asked abruptly, ignoring her question.

"Because I don't like to be manhandled. Perhaps your girlfriend does, but it's not my style," Kelly said coldly, taking off her hat to wipe her damp forehead with her forearm.

Something flickered in the deep green depths of Jake's eyes, then disappeared. "So your pretty blond boyfriend uses the soft approach with you." Jake's voice was dangerously silky, his eyes narrowed in contemplation.

"Or is he just cautious of those carefully manicured claws?"

"You said it," Kelly said cockily. "To be perfectly honest," she continued recklessly, "you just don't do anything for me."

In one swift, fluid motion, Jake jumped down from his horse and pulled Kelly down from hers and into his arms. His kiss was savage and punishing, but it did nothing to still the flames licking along her body at his touch. Her arms crept up around his neck as if she were hugging him for dear life. Jake's mouth softened as he sensed her response and drew her into a vortex of spiraling emotions. Kelly's hands raked through the thick strands of Jake's hair, pulling his body even closer against hers.

The hot sun overhead was nothing compared to the heat consuming her body from Jake's caresses. The flint had struck the rock, sparking a burning flame between them. There was no doubt in her mind that Jake wanted her very much. The tense muscles of his body told her that. When Jake finally drew back, Kelly was disconcerted to find her body trembling violently. She gasped, seeing Jake's unbuttoned shirt exposing the muscular, tanned chest. Obviously, during their passionate embrace, she had unbuttoned it to caress the warm, hard skin underneath. She was even more stunned to find her own shirt gaping open and hurriedly closed it, fumbling with buttons that suddenly seemed too large for the buttonholes.

Jake pushed her hands aside, deftly buttoning her shirt, but leaving one button undone to expose the golden-tanned throat. "It's amazing what can happen even when someone doesn't do anything for you," he drawled lazily.

"Why, you—!" Kelly screamed in rage, suddenly seeing the reasoning behind Jake's kiss. She swung out, pounding his chest in anger and totally out of control. She didn't see his hand until it was too late and he had already slapped her cheek. Holding her hand against the stinging skin, she looked up at him with pain and hate in her eyes.

"You were hysterical," Jake said flatly. "It was either that or another method that I think you'd have appreciated even less."

"I hate you." Tears shimmered in her eyes.

"I know." He turned, mounting his horse and waiting for Kelly to do likewise. He looked off into the distance, his face appearing to be carved from teak.

Kelly mounted silently, wondering why Jake was so angry at her words. He was in love with Sheila, so why should he care what she did with her life?

Jake turned the stallion in the direction of the house, walking slowly. When they arrived back at the barn, Jake turned to Will, speaking as if Kelly weren't there. "I'm riding over to the Lonnigans'," he said crisply. "Tell Myrna not to expect me for dinner."

Will looked bewilderedly at Jake's stony features and Kelly's set ones. Whatever had happened during their ride had not been casual or easily forgotten. "Sure," he said slowly.

Kelly led her horse into the barn and woodenly unsaddled the mare, carefully putting the tack away in its place.

"I'll do that for you," Will offered.

Kelly smiled at him faintly. "Thank you, Will, but I'd feel better doing it myself, if you don't mind."

The older man smiled in understanding and walked off, leaving her alone. Kelly stayed in the barn for a long while, slowly grooming the mare and giving her a rubdown. Then she walked slowly up to the house, where she informed an affronted Myrna that she didn't care for any lunch. Kelly changed into her bikini and went out to the pool. After swimming until she felt exhausted, she flopped onto a lounger and promptly fell asleep.

"Well, young lady, if you think you've had a long enough nap, you can get yourself dressed for your dinner." Myrna's tart voice filtered through Kelly's dreams. "I don't allow no half-dressed people at my table. So you go put on something proper."

Yawning, Kelly looked up at the cook's disapproving face. "I'm sorry; I guess I was more tired than I thought."

"Good way to get sunstroke, too," Myrna retorted. "Miz Cassidy says if you didn't mind she'd appreciate your company for dinner in her sitting room."

"Oh, I'd like that." She sat up quickly.

"Then you've got half an hour to get yourself decent," the older woman said over her shoulder as she returned to her kitchen.

Since she didn't have much time, Kelly settled for a quick shower and twisted her hair up on top of her head. Because it was a warm evening, she chose a deep coral silk caftan which showed off her golden tan to its best.

Later, when she knocked on Maureen's door and was instructed to enter, she found the older woman seated at a small table near the window.

"Myrna outdid herself this evening; we're having a soufflé." Maureen greeted her with a smile.

"How are you feeling?"

"Much better. I'm just not a person who enjoys lying around taking it easy when there's so much to be done. My doctor has a wonderful time scolding me."

Kelly's eyes were drawn toward an open door which led to the bedroom. Glancing in, she couldn't help but see a huge, old-fashioned four-poster bed with a delicately embroidered cover.

"How beautiful," she breathed in awe. "How old is it?"

"One hundred and fifty years." There was a ring of pride in Maureen's voice. "John's grandmother brought it over from Ireland. John was born in that bed. And so was Jake." Her shoulders shook with laughter. "He was two weeks early, and when he decided to be born he didn't waste any time."

"No, I guess he wouldn't," Kelly whispered,

moving into the bedroom and letting her fingers caress the smooth wood. Try as she might, she couldn't imagine Jake as a tiny, defenseless baby.

"I can imagine this seems old-fashioned and sentimental to a modern young woman like you."

Kelly shook her head in denial. "I'm not as modern as some people think I am," she said sadly.

Maureen shot her a curious look but said nothing. Over dinner she questioned Kelly extensively about her life in New York. "Don't you have one special boyfriend?"

"No one special," Kelly said honestly as her mind tripped backward, thinking of the men she had dated over the past few months.

"Do you want to keep on with your career, Kelly?" Maureen asked softly. "Are you and your brother going to model those clothes for years to come?"

"Kyle has a master's degree in journalism. Under a pseudonym he writes very popular murder mysteries. He has no worries. As for me, I'll just wait and see."

Kelly found herself becoming evasive as Maureen began questioning her about her family. She badly wanted to blurt out her father's story, but she knew that this would not be the time, not with Maureen looking so frail and tired. After dinner, noticing the older woman's wan features, Kelly suggested that Maureen retire for the evening. After bidding her good night, Kelly decided to find a book in the library. Glancing through the shelves, she finally selected a novel and curled up in a nearby chair. Soon she was engrossed in the modern-day adventure story. But the previous night's lack of sleep, counterbalanced only by the short nap that afternoon, eventually caught up with her and her eyelids drooped more and more until they finally closed and her head flopped back against the chair.

The sounds of shouting woke Kelly up. Turning over on her side, she pulled her blanket over her shoulders, sleepily frowning against the intrusion on her sleep. Suddenly she felt that something was very wrong and her eyes flew open. She was lying on her bed, fully dressed, with a blanket over her.

How had that happened? The last thing she remembered was sitting in the library reading. How had she gotten here if she had fallen asleep in the library? Unless . . . Oh, no! Had Jake carried her to her room and covered her up? Kelly's cheeks burned at the thought of Jake seeing her asleep. Getting out of bed, she realized that Jake had also taken off her shoes.

"I'm surprised he left my clothes on," she muttered to herself.

After showering and donning a fresh change of clothes, Kelly headed for the dining room. She was surprised to find Jake at the table, calmly drinking coffee.

"Good morning." He barely looked up from the letter he was reading.

"Morning," Kelly mumbled, heading for the sideboard to pour herself a cup of coffee.

Seating herself at the table, she looked sharply at Jake. "Did you put me on my bed last night?"

"You looked pretty uncomfortable in that chair when I got home, so I carried you to your room, yes."

A smile touched Kelly's lips. It was difficult for her to imagine anyone picking up her five-foot-seven frame and carrying her anywhere. She was also suddenly flooded through with a warm feeling that she quickly denied. "I'm glad you take your vitamins," she murmured, acidly sweet. "I'm sure that carrying me is a change from carrying people who are a great deal smaller."

Jake lifted his head to look directly into Kelly's deep turquoise eyes. "Actually, from the way you snuggled up against me when I picked you up, I figured you didn't care to be put down. In fact, when I did put you down, you didn't seem to want to let go. It was as if you wanted me to join you." Kelly's face flamed under his mocking eyes.

"I'm surprised, then, that you didn't undress me, too," she finally replied.

Jake dabbed his mouth with his napkin as he rose to his feet. "I might have thought of it," he said softly. "But I make it a habit not to seduce young women who are difficult to wake up. Perhaps I should contact your boyfriend and find out his method."

"That might be a good idea," she snapped. "Maybe it would work on Sheila, too."

Jake's eyes hardened at Kelly's flippant words, but he said nothing. Picking up his hat from a nearby chair, he left the room, his boots ringing on the polished wood of the hallway floor. The slam of the front door came moments later.

"If my cake falls because of your foul temper, Jake Cassidy, you're going to get a tongue-lashing you'll never forget." Mryna's voice carried across the yard. Jake's reply was inaudible.

After finishing her coffee, Kelly picked up the remaining dishes and carried them into the kitchen.

"Now, that's my job. You just go on and make sure that stubborn woman doesn't overtire herself," Myrna ordered.

Walking back along the hall to Maureen's sitting room, Kelly reflected on how easily she was fitting into this household. When she had to leave, she was going to find it a painful wrench.

Maureen was dressed in a deep blue lounging robe, with a needlepoint canvas lying in her lap. "I just had a phone call from Mrs. Lonnigan. It seems we've been invited there for dinner this evening," she said casually. "They're looking forward to meeting you."

"Obviously little Sheila wants to show me her property again," Kelly said dryly, going on to explain what she meant when she saw Maureen's puzzled frown. "Jake."

"Ah, yes." Maureen nodded her head in understanding. "Sheila has been after Jake for so long I've almost lost track of time. I guess in the long run she'll win out and he'll marry her." But there was a strange note in her voice and she looked quizzically at Kelly as she spoke.

Why did those words send a pain thrusting through Kelly's body? She couldn't care less what happened to Jake, right?

"Dinner will be casual over there, so you won't have to worry about dressing up," Maureen told her, adding dryly, "Sheila wants to consider it a family-style dinner."

One thing Kelly had always been adept at was packing an extensive wardrobe. The last thing she was going to do was show up at the Lonnigan house in casual clothes. Not once did it occur to her that she was deliberately baiting Sheila's anger and tantalizing Jake.

That evening, when Kelly walked down the hallway toward the living room, she could hear the murmuring of voices. Jake and his mother, she guessed easily and accurately. For a moment Kelly hesitated, wondering if she had gone too far in choosing the strapless black silk jumpsuit and a multicolored loose jacket whose tails tied at her waist. The strappy silver heels she wore only added to her regal height. She had left her hair loose, one side held back with a red comb.

When Kelly entered the living room, Jake's back was to her. Maureen was facing her, though, and the older woman's eyes danced as she set down her glass of sherry.

"I'm sorry if I've kept you waiting," Kelly spoke up.

When Jake turned, the impatience in his face disappeared as he gazed at the beautiful young woman. "I thought Sheila specified that tonight was to be just a casual dinner," he commented.

"Oh?" Kelly was all wide-eyed innocence. "I'm sorry. Perhaps I should go back and change."

"No, we're late enough as it is," Jake muttered, swallowing the rest of his whiskey and stubbing out his cigarette in the ashtray. "The car's out front. Let's get going."

In the close confines of the car, Kelly's seductive perfume blended easily with Jake's musky aftershave. Maureen hung back deliberately, so that Kelly was forced to sit between mother and son in the front seat; close enough for her to feel the warmth of Jake's body.

Sheila herself answered the door, looking beautiful in a sheer bronze caftan with a deep brown silk underslip. Her eyes narrowed as she took in Kelly's bright beauty.

"We're so pleased you could join us for dinner, Kelly." Sheila's tones were honeyed. "And how do you like our poor, barren country?"

"I enjoy it immensely," Kelly said sincerely, not seeing the studying gaze she received from Jake at her answer. "The peace and quiet are heavenly after the noisy city."

Sheila's parents were warm and friendly people whose interest in Kelly's modeling career was genuine. Kelly silently wondered how such sincere people could have such a calculating daughter as Sheila. Throughout the evening, the auburn-haired woman seemed bent on showing Kelly that she and Jake were more than just neighbors. Every gesture, every exchange of glances, and her subtle emphasis of certain words were all designed to have intimate undertones.

"Will you be here for our Summer Cup, Kelly?" Sheila asked. "We have an old-fashioned gala; it's one of our biggest social events of the year, with horse races and various other games."

"Actually, my vacation is going by faster than I like. I have to be back in New York by the tenth of next month. But I hope so."

"How trying it must be to have to constantly watch your weight," Sheila drawled, her hazel eyes glinting with malice. "Oh, of course, you do get a great many other things to make up for it. Traveling all over the world, wearing beautiful clothes, meeting fascinating people."

"Posing under hot lights for long stretches of time, looking happy and carefree whether I feel that way or not," Kelly countered. "Wearing summer clothes in the winter and having to pose outside and almost freeze. I'm not saying I don't enjoy it. Just that there are a great many drawbacks most people don't realize."

"What about that gorgeous man they always show you with?" Sheila leaned forward. "The two of you seem to have such a warm rapport."

"Kyle is warm, generous, intelligent, and charming," she said, deliberately keeping her eyes on Jake. "The kind of man any woman would want."

Kelly was secretly relieved when Jake announced that they would have to be going because of the late hour. As Maureen and Kelly walked outside with Mr. and Mrs. Lonnigan, Sheila kept Jake back for a few moments, much to Kelly's amusement. When they finally walked outside, Sheila clung to Jake's arm, looking smug.

"Donald and Mary are such warm people," Maureen commented during the drive home. "Sometimes I wonder . . ." Her voice abruptly dropped off.

Not wanting to sound catty, Kelly stayed silent. When Jake parked the car in front of the house and helped the two women out, Kelly murmured a quick good night and hurried inside.

She easily dropped off to sleep, waking up only once in the middle of the night, when she felt as if she were being observed. Propping herself up on one elbow, she looked around the dark room and out onto the veranda beyond the open French doors. Her forehead creased in a frown; she was unable to understand what had woken her up. Since she didn't hear anything, she lay back down and soon fell asleep again until morning.

Chapter Four

Kelly saw little of Jake over the next few days, and when she did, his eyes seemed to look through her instead of at her. The few times he spoke to her, his words were abrupt and impersonal. For some odd reason, his actions hurt her.

One evening Maureen was sitting in the den, watching television and doing her needlepoint; she was replacing a worn-out chair cushion in the dining room. Kelly was sitting on the couch to better see the brilliant pattern of purple pansies against a cream-colored background.

"Using velvet yarn instead of the regular wool gives them the soft effect you see in real pansies," Maureen explained. "I know they're not practical, but I love the design and colors."

Suddenly Kelly heard her name and she looked up, surprised to see her own face on the television screen and hear the announcer introducing a short interview with Kelly and Kyle James, the new symbols for Pegasus Designs. Kelly remembered the interview; it had been filmed several months earlier.

"How wonderful!" Maureen said happily, looking up.

Concentrating on the television program, the two women didn't see Jake standing in the doorway, leaning against the doorjamb, his eyes intent on the screen.

"Kelly and Kyle are the two newest stars in the fashion world today," the announcer continued. "These twins are well known for their sunny dispositions and easygoing natures." There followed a brief discussion, with both Kelly and Kyle taking part, about the current fashion scene and modeling as a career.

Just as the interview ended, Kelly heard a sound and looked up in time to see Jake turning in the doorway to stride away. Suddenly upset for reasons she didn't want to examine, Kelly excused herself to Maureen and left the room. She didn't see the man leaning against the wall of the hallway, and she gasped in fright as a hand gripped her arm and spun her against a hard surface—Jake's chest.

"Why didn't you tell me that he's your brother?" he growled in her ear.

"You—you didn't ask me," Kelly said breathlessly, conscious of being at eye level with the open throat of Jake's shirt.

"You must have enjoyed letting me think he was your lover. All those cute little comments you let drop about your love life were really great," he said harshly. "You really got your kicks, didn't you?"

"Why should you care?" Kelly asked huskily, lifting her eyes to his. "I don't mean anything to you. You called me just about every name in the book, and I figured that worse wouldn't be long in coming."

"I should strangle you." Jake's hands lifted to encircle her throat, his grip slowly tightening against her soft skin. The dark look on his face was frightening.

Kelly's breath caught in her throat as she anticipated his punishment. She felt as if time had been suspended. Jake's eyes narrowed to emerald slits, his expression unreadable. The lean fingers momentarily tightened again, then relaxed. His hands dropped to his sides.

"I don't know if he's luckier being your brother than he was when I thought he was your lover," Jake said finally. "Get out of here."

Kelly backed away, her eyes refusing to leave Jake's face. She didn't understand this new side of this complex man. She hadn't thought he'd be so angry over her deception, which, after all, could hardly matter to him.

"I always thought you were a lying little cheat. Now I know I'm right," Jake said harshly as he watched her go.

"Our truce is over," Kelly said tautly before she fled for the safety of the den.

Jake followed her into the room, but with his mother still seated on the couch he was unable to continue their tense conversation.

Kelly chattered nervously to Maureen as Jake walked over to the bar and splashed a generous amount of whiskey into a glass before flopping down in a nearby chair. He had deliberately picked a chair which gave him an unobstructed view of Kelly's face. As he sipped his drink, Jake's eyes never left her face, focusing especially closely on her lips. Kelly had never known a man who could unnerve her the way Jake did. She had to steel herself not to blush under his hooded gaze.

"I—I had completely forgotten about that television interview," Kelly told Maureen. "It was taped several months ago."

"I must say, your brother has quite a sense of humor." Maureen chuckled. As she continued talking, Jake's face grew darker.

With a minimum of movement, Jake was out of his chair and at the bar, pouring himself another drink without seeing the disapproving look his mother shot him.

"I—I think I'll go to bed now," Kelly murmured, anxious to get away from Jake's probing eyes.

"Good night." Maureen picked up her needlepoint.

Jake said nothing, but his eyes spoke volumes to Kelly as she left the den.

Inside her bedroom, Kelly undressed, slipping on a peach-colored silk nightgown with lace sleeves. She stood before the mirror, brushing her hair.

"What's happening to me?" she whispered to herself later as she lay in bed. "Why should I care what some dirty, sweaty cowboy thinks of me or my life-style? What does it matter?" Then as she recalled that episode in Jake's office, Kelly realized that she knew the answer only too well.

She drifted off to sleep, but not for long. Lying in bed, she sighed out loud; she was wide awake and without a hope of getting back to sleep. Since she didn't believe in taking drugs to sleep, Kelly decided that the best medicine for her would be a glass of warm milk. Getting out of bed, she slipped on a sheer lacy robe and crept out of her room, heading for the kitchen. Kelly had become so used to the house that she could find her way easily in the dark.

After fixing her warm milk, Kelly sat down at the kitchen table to drink it. She silently wondered how Kyle would like this easygoing life. She smiled to herself, knowing that her energetic and fun-loving twin wouldn't enjoy this quiet, leisurely pace at all. During the few vacations they had spent together, Kyle had been constantly chafing to go out somewhere, to seek the nightlife.

"What the—!"

Kelly turned in surprise to see Jake standing in the doorway. "I couldn't sleep," she said defensively, gesturing toward her glass. "I came out to fix myself some warm milk." Feeling uneasy under Jake's steady, unnerving gaze, she snapped, "Don't worry, I'll clean up after myself, if that's what you're so upset about."

"If anyone would be upset, it would be Myrna," he said evenly, entering the kitchen. Jake opened a cabinet door to take out a glass, which he filled with water from the tap. Then he turned around to lean against the counter, holding the glass in one strong hand. "The early hours we keep must be a strain for you," he commented.

"Actually, I'm not much of a night person," Kelly admitted, watching in fascination as Jake leaned his head back to swallow the water, the muscles in his throat standing out. "I enjoy curling up in bed with a book more than going out dancing."

His deep emerald eyes traveled over her honey-colored, sleep-tousled hair and the pale peach nightgown he could see beneath the sheer robe. Kelly flushed under Jake's probing gaze as she realized how quiet the house was and how late the hour. The crazy thought entered her head that this scene would be very different if they were married, or even lovers. She wouldn't have to worry about reading a book or drinking warm milk to help her to sleep. She wouldn't need either with Jake lying beside her. Kelly hurriedly lowered her lashes to hide the expression in her eyes. Then she rose quickly to her feet, picking up her glass and approaching the sink. Jake kept his eyes on her flushed face. Because he refused to move from his spot, she was forced to brush past him to rinse out her glass. The warmth of his body reached out to her as she turned on the faucet.

"Very pretty," Jake said idly.

Kelly's head snapped up in confusion to catch him gazing raptly at her state of undress. He moved a hand and let his fingers trace the rounded neckline of her robe. This quietly sensual side of him was new and almost frightening to her.

"I want to thank you for being so kind to my mother." Jake's low voice was hypnotic.

"She's come to enjoy your company very much."

"It's not difficult. She's a warm and loving person, and I'm very fond of her," Kelly said honestly.

"But not of her son."

"I didn't think it mattered to you." Kelly found her hand beginning to tremble as she set the glass down in the sink.

"And if it did?"

Kelly nervously twisted her hands together. "Look, I don't know why you started this conversation, but I don't see any need for it to continue. So I think I'll go back to bed."

"What are you scared of?" Jake's voice was deliberately taunting as he straightened up. He suddenly looked very tall and dangerous as he walked slowly toward her as she retreated. "Are you scared of *me*, Kelly?" This time his voice was curiously gentle as her retreat was halted by the table behind her.

"Of course not!" Her eyes were wary as Jake's finger traced the outline of her mouth with a feather-light touch. "Don't, Jake." Her voice was forced from her throat. Kelly's eyes had darkened to a deep turquoise at the strange feelings Jake's touch was evoking.

Jake bent down, his lips following the path his finger had taken in a light and tender kiss. Kelly was totally unprepared for this unexpected gentleness after the harsh kisses he had subjected her to earlier. She didn't want his tenderness. She didn't want him at all! Jake's hand on her breast was softly rubbing the rounded mound under the soft silk and lace. Uttering a choked cry, Kelly wrenched herself out of Jake's arms and ran out of the kitchen.

Her eyes blurred by tears, Kelly wasn't careful as she ran down the dark hallway. One bare foot slipped on the polished wood and she slid into a small table. Crying out, she fell, hitting the side of her face against the table edge.

"Kelly!" The dark hallway was suddenly bathed in light and Jake was instantly by her side. "Are you all right?" he asked in a concerned voice, framing her face with his hands.

She winced at the pain shooting along the side of her face but refused to show it. "I'm fine." She bit out the words, pulling Jake's hands from her face. "Just leave me alone." Kelly gripped the side of the table, refusing to grasp his extended hand. Pulling herself up, Kelly stepped forward, only to feel a shooting pain pierce her forehead. "Jake," she moaned wildly, reaching out before a black abyss swallowed her.

Later, when Kelly came to, she was lying on her bed. She slowly turned her head, involuntarily crying out at the sharp pains in her temple. She put up a hand as if to brush away the needles piercing her face.

"Easy." The side of the bed shifted downward as a heavy weight came down next to her. Jake took her hand away from her face and grasped it between his own two palms.

"My—my face hurts," Kelly whispered.

"You fell against the table," Jake said quietly. "You gave me quite a scare when you didn't want to wake up. I called the doctor; you may have a concussion."

Kelly started to move until another sharp pain shot through her head, bringing a whimper to her lips.

"Now, don't move." His voice was soothing as he gently pushed damp strands of her hair away from her face, still holding her hand in one of his. "Can you try to sleep until the doctor comes?" Jake asked quietly.

"Will you stay with me until he does?" Kelly was enjoying the warm feeling of his hand covering hers.

Jake flashed her a reassuring smile, which softened the harsh planes of his face. "I'll stay."

Comforted, Kelly smiled faintly, and her dark, thick lashes settled down on her pale cheeks.

When Kelly's eyes next opened, Jake was gone from the room; he had been replaced by a kindly-faced man in his late sixties and an obviously worried Maureen.

"Glad to see you decided to join us, young lady," the older man told her. "You're very lucky that the skin wasn't broken. I understand from Maureen that your face is your fortune, so to speak."

"It hurts a lot," Kelly replied. "I feel as if I was shot full of novocaine and now it's wearing off."

"You just have a nasty bruise and quite a black eye. I don't think you have a concussion, though." The doctor patted Kelly's hand, and she decided immediately that she liked this warm and friendly man. "I'm leaving some pain pills for you because I imagine you're going to feel uncomfortable for the next few days. I suggest you stay in bed for a couple days, at least, until the dizziness wears off." He rose to his feet. "I have no doubts that, with Maureen here to take care of you, you'll be fine. I'm also going to give you a sedative before I leave." Kelly could feel a faint prick in her arm as he administered the hypodermic.

"I'll see you out," Maureen said quietly.

As she cautiously shifted her head, Kelly could see the warm expression in the doctor's eyes as he looked at Maureen. It was obvious that he hoped to be more than just her friend. Then, wincing at the jabbing pains the movement had caused, Kelly lay still until Maureen returned.

"You certainly gave Jake quite a fright." The older woman smiled as she smoothed the coverlet. "When you didn't come to right away, he burst into my room as if the devil himself was at his heels. It's lucky that Jake heard you when you stumbled."

It was obvious that Jake hadn't told his mother the truth about Kelly's accident, and Kelly decided not to correct her. Her brilliant turquoise eyes grew heavy with sleep from the injection the doctor had given her and Maureen's face became blurred.

"I feel so tired." Even her voice sounded thick. Kelly's breathing became even as she slipped into a deep, drug-induced sleep.

Kelly slept so heavily that she was unaware of the broad-shouldered figure lounging in a chair near her bed. Deep emerald eyes never left her face, noting the delicate cheekbones, one bearing the deep purple marks of a bruise, the dark, thick lashes feathering the golden skin, the stubborn jawline, and the sculptured nose no plastic surgeon had ever touched.

When Kelly woke up again, bright afternoon sunshine was filtering through the drawn drapes. The sharp pain in her forehead had finally subsided to a dull throb. The chair was pulled up near her bed, a sleeping Jake sprawled against the cushions.

"Jake," Kelly softly ventured, almost hating to wake him.

He was awake in an instant, leaning forward to grasp her outstretched hand. "You're beginning to look more like yourself." He grinned.

Kelly was surprised by the lines of strain etched around his mouth. Had they been caused by her accident? Had he been that worried about her?

"Do you still have any pain?" he asked.

"Not as bad. It's dulled quite a bit." Kelly managed a faint smile. "You look terrible, though."

"I'll be O.K. now that I know you're feeling better." Jake grinned, rubbing his hand over his unshaven jaw. "The doctor said you could have some soup if you're hungry. He figures it might hurt for you to chew anything solid. Want to try some now?"

Kelly started to nod her head until a sharp pain reminded her of the reason she was lying in bed during the afternoon. Jake's eyes narrowed as he noted her wince.

"I'm not used to being sick," she explained, slowly attempting to sit up.

Jake quickly moved forward to help her by plumping up the pillows behind her. Kelly's breath constricted at Jake's nearness, the clean, woodsy scent of his aftershave, and the sharp tang of the cigarettes he smoked. He looked down at her upturned face with that unnerving gaze of his focused on her lips.

"The doctor said I was lucky that I came away with only bruises," Kelly whispered. "Do I look very bad? That is, as bad as I feel?"

Jake smiled, understanding that her question had nothing to do with vanity. "You could never look bad to me," he replied huskily. "Why don't I get you some supper." In a moment he was gone.

Kelly wondered what her face looked like, but she soon discovered that getting out of bed to catch a peek in the dresser mirror only brought on fresh pain.

She was disappointed when Maureen was the one who brought in a tray holding a bowl of soup and a cup of tea.

"I'm sorry to put you to so much trouble," Kelly murmured as Maureen set the tray on her lap.

"Nonsense," the older woman said briskly. "I enjoy having someone to coddle. Usually the only times I have someone to spoil are when my grandchildren come for a visit. Then I have my hands full."

"You miss them, don't you?"

"Very much." The older woman's eyes were misty. "There are times when I wish Jake would—" Her voice dropped off abruptly. "Well, I should let you rest. If you need anything, call out."

Kelly thought that, after all the sleep she had gotten, she would lie awake, but it wasn't long before her eyelids slowly drooped shut. She stirred some time later, hazily aware of a tall figure standing by her bed. Smiling faintly, Kelly reached out to grope for the strong hand, lacing her fingers through his. Comforted, she fell back asleep.

When Kelly woke up the following morning, she felt more like herself. Cautiously sitting up, she swung her legs over the edge of the bed and slowly stood up. After the prickling feeling went away in her legs, she took tiny, hesitant steps toward the bathroom.

"So far, so good," she muttered to herself.

She wanted to comb out the tangled snarls in her hair, so she picked up her brush and moved to the mirror. Her eyes widened in horror as she gazed transfixed at her reflection in the mirror. One cheekbone was mottled black and purple, as was one eye, the deep turquoise depths looking ludicrous amid the swollen skin. Her fingertips brushed lightly against her cheek as if she were hoping that it was only paint that could easily be wiped away.

"No," she moaned. "Oh, no." She collapsed in a heap on the floor, crying in earth-shattering sobs.

"Kelly! Oh, Kelly." Jake's voice was tender, his hands gentle as he gathered her into his strong arms, cradling her against him. He rested his cheek against her hair, making soft crooning noises.

"I look so ugly!" she sobbed, burying her face against his neck as she clung to him. "Why didn't you tell me how horrible I look?"

"Because you don't look ugly to me." He stood up and carried her back to the bed. After settling her among the pillows and straightening the covers around her, Jake sat on the edge of the bed and flashed her a wicked grin. "Actually, you look pretty cute with a black eye."

"Cute!" Kelly dismissed his words with an audible sniff. "I look like something out of a horror film."

"I never thought of you as a vain woman." Jake's voice was reproving. "Do your looks mean that much to you?"

"How can you bear to even look at me?" she demanded.

"Because I see all of you, not just your face. Soon the swelling will go down and the bruises will disappear. Look at the bright side." His voice turned teasing. "You can tell people you put up quite a fight."

Unable to resist Jake's easy charm, Kelly managed a faint smile. "You're not going to allow me to lie here and feel sorry for myself, are you?"

"How did you spend your time in New York?" Jake quickly changed the subject. "Surely you didn't pose in front of the cameras all of the time."

"No. I went to an exercise club two or three times a week, went horseback riding, cleaned my apartment. Sometimes I took a class at the university." Kelly smiled wryly. "I bet you thought I spent all my free time in beauty salons. Well, my hairdresser only sees me every three months for a trim or if I need to have my hair done for a special occasion. My nails are manicured twice a month, and I get a facial once a month to clean out the city's grime and pollution. To be frank, I have better ways of spending my time." Kelly looked toward the open drapes and spied the bright sunshine; she was surprised that Jake was inside during the middle of the day. "Shouldn't you be out with your men?"

"Trying to get rid of me, are you?" Jake teased, rising to his feet. "All right, I get the message. I'll see you this evening at dinner. We'll take a walk afterwards to let you get some fresh air."

Kelly was grateful that Maureen came in later to brush her hair so that she didn't have to look in the mirror again. She silently thought that Jake might have had a hand in that. Although she wasn't vain at heart, seeing the bruises all along one side of her face had been a shock.

That evening Kelly sat in the dining room for the evening meal. She had carefully applied makeup to her face to minimize the effect of the discolored skin, and the rose-colored silk shirt she wore with her black jeans helped bring some of her natural color back into her cheeks.

After dinner Jake excused them to his mother and steered Kelly outside. He took her hand and they walked along the pathway toward the corrals. Kelly looked around to the sprawling house and the nearby barns and felt a warm happiness steal through her body. She couldn't remember ever having felt such a sense of belonging as she did here. Then she remembered that, all too soon, it would be time for her to leave. She would go back to her hectic schedule, the photography sessions, and the life that had now become like a dream to her, a dream of her past.

"Why the sad face?" Jake asked quietly, seeing the fleeting unhappiness in her expression.

"I'm just remembering that it won't be too much longer before my vacation will be over and I'll be a working girl again." She tried to keep her voice light and not let her sorrow show. "Of course, no one ever wants to see their vacation end and have to return home."

It was a long time before Jake spoke. "No, I guess not," he said finally. "Look, I wanted to talk to you alone to tell you that I'm sorry for what happened that night. If I hadn't frightened you, you probably wouldn't have fallen and hurt yourself." He took matches and cigarettes out of his shirt pocket and bent his head down to light one. He drew deeply on the cigarette as he replaced the pack in his shirt pocket. "I've cursed myself a thousand times since that night," he said grimly.

Kelly turned around to lean on the fence, resting her chin on her folded arms on the top rail. She knew it took a great deal for someone as proud as Jake to humbly apologize. It was something that he had obviously been thinking about for some time. Not long ago, Kelly would have gloated over this moment, but no more.

"My own stubborn streak didn't help any," Kelly said ruefully. "My mother used to tell me that I'd get in trouble if I ran around without looking where I was going. Little did I know how right she was." She laughed softly.

The hair on the back of Kelly's neck prickled, signaling that Jake was standing directly behind her.

"You're not the same woman who arrived here not long ago," Jake commented quietly.

"Oh? Because I've gotten a good tan?" she asked lightly to mask the turmoil her body was undergoing at Jake's nearness.

"Sometimes it's as if you've always been here. You just seem to fit in around the house." His finger moved along the soft strands of her hair as if savoring the smooth tresses. "When I see you talking to my mother, when I see her teaching you needlepoint in the evenings, it all seems so right."

Unable to stand the electric contact, Kelly spun around, forgetting for a moment how close Jake was to her. She tipped her head back, trying without success to read the expression in the dark emerald eyes. Undaunted by her move, Jake's hand slid around to touch her cheek in a feather-light caress.

"Like silk," he mused, keeping his eyes intently on her upturned face. "Smooth and cool to the touch, yet so soft."

Kelly held her breath, waiting for the kiss that must follow this. "Jake?" Her breathless voice was questioning. Waiting.

Jake's body stilled as he gazed down at her face. It was as if he were fighting a battle within himself.

"I promised my mother I wouldn't keep you out too long." His unexpected answer filled Kelly with disappointment. "I also have a pile of paperwork waiting for me in my office and I need to get it done tonight, so we should be getting back."

"Yes, of course," Kelly murmured, unwilling to let her disappointment show.

As they slowly walked back up to the house Kelly was very much aware of Jake's warm hand at the back of her waist. Five minutes later, he deposited Kelly in Maureen's care and murmured an excuse about work to be done in his office. The younger woman was unaware of how openly her disappointment showed after Jake had left the room.

"Shall we finish that chair cover?" Maureen asked quietly, picking up the large square of canvas.

"Why not?" Kelly sighed, accepting the fabric and rummaging through the large canvas tote bag for the bright green wool she had been using to make the leaves on the floral chair cover.

Two days later, Kelly reclined on a chaise longue by the pool. Since she didn't plan on swimming, she had chosen pale blue jogging shorts and a matching T-shirt banded in lavender. Still self-conscious about her black eye, even though there was no one about, she wore her oversized sunglasses to hide the vivid discoloration. A large pitcher, filled with fruit juice, and a glass sat on the table near her elbow.

"Well, hello."

Kelly looked up from her magazine to see Sheila cross the patio, chic in her dark gold pants and matching short-sleeved silk shirt. It was not a typical outfit for every day—unless you were visiting someone special.

"Myrna said you were out here resting." Sheila spoke in a silky voice that didn't fool Kelly for one moment. The other woman settled herself in a nearby chair, looking sharply at Kelly's face as if trying to see beyond the dark glasses. "There was a mention in town of your being in some kind of an accident. I thought I'd come by to see how you're feeling. I gather it wasn't anything serious."

"Oh, well, thank you for your concern." Kelly smiled innocently. "What a nice surprise. I thought you'd head down to the barns. Where Jake is, that is."

The other woman's eyes narrowed fractionally. "I never did see you as the wide-eyed innocent some others around here do." Sheila leaned forward in her chair. "You may get what you want when you're in the States because you have a pretty face, but out here your famous name doesn't mean very much. What's puzzling me is how you barged in here and wangled an invitation to stay with the Cassidys. They don't take kindly to strangers. Especially Americans."

"I met Jake when my car broke down," Kelly said, deciding that it was safest to stick to a familiar lie. "He introduced me to Maureen, and they invited me to spend the rest of my vacation with them." She put aside her magazine and leaned forward. "Why are you so nervous about my being here, Sheila? Afraid I'll spirit Jake away right out from under your nose?"

"I have no doubts about Jake," Sheila said confidently. "After all, a city girl like you couldn't fit into this community. What would *you* know about living on a cattle station?"

"I never claimed to know anything about it," Kelly replied calmly as she rose to her feet. "Well, if you'll excuse me, I think I'll go inside now. The sun is getting much too bright out here. I still have to be careful."

"Sheila, I thought that was your car I saw along the side of the house." Jake walked toward the two women, looking masculine and virile in his dusty jeans and denim shirt and carrying his hat by the brim. As he sensed the antagonism in the air between them, his eyes darted warily toward Kelly, whose expression was hidden by her sunglasses. The slowly disappearing bruises on her cheekbone had been disguised by the skillful use of makeup until nothing showed except to the trained eye.

"Oh, I'm glad you're here, Jake," Kelly said sweetly. "Sheila really came over to see you, and, as I was just going in, she won't be alone." She leaned down to pick up her magazine. As she bent over, her sunglasses slipped down, revealing her bruised eye.

Sheila looked at her half in shock, half in malicious amusement. "Oh, you poor dear," she clucked insincerely. "Did you run into a door?"

Kelly merely smiled as she slid her sunglasses back up on her nose. Walking slowly, with an exaggerated swing to her hips, she approached Jake and reached up to pat his cheek.

"Jake is such a sweetie." She turned toward a fuming Sheila. "But there are times when he can be so *physical*, if you know what I mean." Her hips still swinging, Kelly walked into the house, her long slim legs golden beneath her shorts. She smiled to herself as she heard Sheila's demanding voice.

"What does she mean, Jake?"

Completely satisfied with herself, Kelly opened the sliding glass door leading to the den.

"You really opened a can of worms there." Myrna's amused voice momentarily startled Kelly.

"You were eavesdropping," she accused,

but she smiled to take any sting out of her words.

"And enjoying every minute of it," Myrna said, unabashed. "You know, of course, that you've made an enemy in that one. She won't appreciate your playing pattycake with someone she considers her property."

Kelly turned back to observe Sheila's tense face as she talked to a nonchalant Jake. "She certainly doesn't look pleased with Jake's explanation," she commented idly.

"He can be a very surprising man," Myrna threw over her shoulder as she left the room.

Kelly stood near the sliding door to watch the two people outside. Jake's tenderness toward her over the past few days had surprised her. His warmth was both unexpected and scary. Jake was indeed a complex man, and a very appealing one.

The aura of sensuality that surrounded him was rapidly drawing Kelly into its intricate web. Many times she would find his eyes on her face, moving over her as if he were physically caressing her. The trouble was, Kelly would find herself wishing that he was indeed touching her with his hands instead of his eyes. His raw virility was something new to her, and she was rapidly becoming addicted to him. Withdrawal would be more painful than any torture known to man or woman. In the future, no matter who had his arms around her, Kelly knew she would think of the black-haired Australian who had raised such deep passion in her.

Kelly knew she couldn't stay much longer with the Cassidys or her feelings for Jake would be sure to be revealed. Even if she never got a chance to explain to Maureen about her real reason for being there, she had to leave.

Chapter Five

One afternoon the two women were sitting by the pool, Kelly wearing a sea-green one-piece bathing suit with a narrow halter strap. In a hesitant voice, she mentioned making plans for returning home.

"Oh, no, you can't leave yet," Maureen protested. "The Summer Rodeo begins next week. Not to mention the gala. You must stay for that. After all, you did say you don't have to return to New York until the tenth of next month."

Kelly sat cross-legged on the lounger, knowing that the time had come for her to tell Maureen her real reason for being there, no matter what that would do to the tenuous regard Jake was beginning to feel for her.

"Maureen, I—I'm not sure how to tell you this." She felt at a loss for words. "But I lied to you. I'm not here on vacation. Actually, I had my vacation all planned; I was going to go to Jamaica. Then my father had a heart attack and was hospitalized. The last time I saw him before he died, he told me about meeting a nurse's aide during the war while he was in New Zealand. How she bullied him into walking again when he had no desire to, and how he fell in love with her." Kelly hesitated.

"What else did your father tell you?" the older woman prompted softly.

"How he asked her to marry him and she accepted. And then how an argument caused them to break up. My father was soon sent back to the United States and given a medical discharge. But he never forgot the woman. He knew he still loved her, and he wrote her a letter telling her so, and that he still wanted to marry her. But the mails were delayed or something, and when Daddy didn't hear from her he thought that she didn't love him, after all. When he finally did receive a letter from her, he had already married someone else. So he had to write to her to say he had married. He never forgot her, though, and somehow managed to keep track of her over the years. He wanted to see her again after he found out that her husband died, but he was afraid she would refuse to see him." Kelly raised her misty eyes to see that Maureen's were as tear-filled as her own.

"At first I didn't know what to say to him," Maureen said softly. "I couldn't even remember what we had argued about in the first place. I did know I loved Ross, though, and I finally wrote to tell him so. Unfortunately, I was too late. Then I met John, and he helped heal the wounds."

Kelly slipped off the lounger and walked over to Maureen to kneel on the ground by her chair. "Daddy told me how it hurt him to write to you saying that he had married. He thought that you hadn't loved him, and he didn't know what to do," Kelly said earnestly. "At first it hurt me to think that my father had loved someone else more than he loved my mother. I could tell by the way he looked when he said your name how much you had meant, still meant, to him. I'll be honest in saying that I didn't want to come here. But Daddy wanted you to know that he hadn't forgotten you or thought of you as one of those wartime romances. I wanted to tell you all this in the beginning. I even sent you a note when I arrived in Sydney, but Jake somehow intercepted it and came to see me when I got to the Outback. He said it was harmful to bring up the past and—"

"Damn you!" A harsh voice exploded from the other side of the pool.

Kelly stood up and turned to face Jake's dark and angry features. "You had to, didn't you?" he ground out. "You little—"

"Jake!" Maureen's normally soft voice cut through the air with the sharpness of a whip. She stood up and put a comforting arm around Kelly's shoulders. "I've known that Kelly was Ross James's daughter since the first time you brought her here."

Jake looked at his mother as if unable to believe his ears.

"Go inside and get changed," Maureen told Kelly. "And please tell Myrna we'll be lunching in town and doing some shopping." She gave the younger woman a gentle push.

Unsure of Jake's volatile temper, Kelly kept

as far away from him as possible as she skirted the pool. As soon as she had disappeared inside, Jake walked toward his mother.

"I can understand your motives for protecting me," Maureen told him. "And I appreciate them. Ross was a long-ago love, and one I could never forget. I wasn't sure why Kelly came here when I first met her, but I had an idea it had something to do with her father. What I'm wondering is why, if you were so afraid of my finding out who her father was and what her motives were for being here, you allowed her to stay here in the house."

"*You* invited her, I didn't," he argued.

"Oh, Jake." Her voice was warm and full of affection for her son. "You, of all people, should know better than to try to pull the wool over my eyes. You must have known that I would be curious about why you brought Kelly out here in the first place. If you really hadn't wanted her here, you would merely have not given her my invitation and told me that she had refused. Yet you brought her out here that first time and, later, to stay. I, for one, think there's another reason."

"I warned her not to tell you," Jake said stubbornly.

"Don't try those tactics with me, because they won't work," Maureen said briskly, a twinkle in her eyes. "I'm sure there's a very good reason why she's still here. She's a beautiful and intelligent woman, and she even seems able to put up with your bullish temper. You're a good-looking man, Jake, and can be quite charming when you want to be. Do something smart for once and don't let her go back to the States."

"It's that obvious, is it?" Jake asked wryly.

"Of course; I'm your mother, remember?" She chuckled. "Start using that fatal Irish charm you inherited from your father. Kelly and I are lunching in town, so I doubt we'll be back before late afternoon. See if you can be more sociable by then."

"Going to put in a good word for me?" He grinned at his mother.

"You're on your own. You don't need my help." Maureen patted his shoulder and kissed him on the cheek. "Now I have to go in and change."

Maureen said nothing about Jake's outburst to Kelly as they drove into town. They had lunch at the hotel, where Maureen was greeted warmly by the various townspeople they met. The older woman insisted on introducing Kelly to everyone, telling them that she was the daughter of an old family friend. Everywhere they went the talk was centered on the upcoming Summer Cup and the costume gala.

"This year is a bit strange, because I've always been on the committee planning the festivities, but this time I just didn't have the energy to do all the work involved." Maureen sighed. She looked at Kelly with a keen eye. "I have a gown in mind for you to wear. It's one I wore when I was much younger and slimmer. I don't think it would need too many alterations, because we're pretty much the same height."

Kelly sighed inwardly, realizing that she would have to stay or else appear ungrateful for refusing the older woman's gracious offers. Maureen seemed to be looking forward to having her stay for the festivities. And Kelly had to admit that it all sounded like a great deal of fun and that she would never have a chance like this again. But she wondered what Jake's reaction would be to her staying on. She figured he would want her to keep as far away from him as possible. Kelly wondered what mother and son had discussed after she had gone into the house, but she doubted that either one would tell her.

Kelly was totally surprised by Jake's change in attitude toward her that evening. During dinner, while far from friendly, he was coolly polite, as if he were far away in his own thoughts.

"Will you be racing Banshee this year?" Maureen asked her son.

"Is that a subtle hint for me not to?"

"Only if you think you're going to break your neck—or your collarbone, like you did two years ago." She turned to Kelly. "If Jake doesn't break a bone at least once every couple of years, I don't think he's happy. He usually does it when he helps break the horses. One year he was thrown into a fence. Broke his shoulder and his wrist. The fool insisted on helping his men catch the horse before he'd agree to be treated." Maureen glared at her son.

Kelly had seen western movies involving the taming of wild horses, and now, hearing firsthand about some of the dangers involved, her face whitened and her fork clattered to her plate. Visions of that magnificent body broken or trampled drove all thoughts of eating from her mind.

"I—I thought your men would break the horses," she said through stiff lips. "That it would take a special talent to work with wild horses."

"It does. But I don't have my men do anything I won't do myself," Jake replied.

Kelly had no appetite for the remainder of the meal. Myrna gave a disapproving sniff a few minutes later when she refused the tasty apple cobbler.

"I have to start watching what I eat," Kelly hastily explained with a short laugh. "Models aren't encouraged to look plump."

"Will said you might want to go down to the barn after you finish your dinner," Myrna told Jake. "Burnished Gold is likely to foal sometime tonight."

Jake dabbed at his mouth with his napkin and dropped it on his plate. Pushing his chair back, he rose to his feet.

"I'm through now. I'm going down to the barn," he told his mother, suddenly angry again and refusing to spare a glance for Kelly. "Goldie took her time foaling last year, so I'm sure she won't be in any hurry this time, either." In a moment he was gone.

Kelly's fingers encircled her wineglass as she studied the shimmering ruby liquid. "Everyone depends on Jake, don't they?" she asked huskily.

"Yes, they do."

"Shouldn't you call a veterinarian? In case something happens to the horse."

"Jake is a qualified vet. That's what he studied at the university. He also knows the quirks of every animal on this land. And Goldie enjoys being coddled and pandered to every chance she gets. Jake knows how to use his charm on her." Maureen smiled. "Tomorrow I'd like you to try on that gown so Myrna and I can see if any alterations need to be made," she continued. "I just know it will look lovely on you."

"I can understand why Daddy loved you so much." Kelly's voice was warm and sincere. "You care about people and you mean every word you say. There're so few people like that in this cynical world."

"I care about those I love," Maureen said simply. "Come on; we might as well continue your needlepoint lessons." For the past few days she had been teaching Kelly various needlepoint stitches, and the younger woman had begun a pillow, finding enjoyment in the simple task which served as therapy for her wandering and confused mind.

After a few hours of helping Kelly with pricked fingers and crooked stitches, Maureen announced she was going to bed.

"I think I'll stay up for a while," Kelly told

her. "If nothing else, needlepoint is teaching me patience." She grinned.

Patting her shoulder, Maureen smiled and walked out of the room, heading for her own bedroom.

Kelly looked down at the partially finished pattern of tiger lilies lying in her lap, debating whether to continue working on it or not. Finally laying it aside, she picked up a book and leafed idly through the pages, unable to keep her mind on the story. Later, when she looked up at the clock, she was surprised to find that it was past midnight and Jake still hadn't come back to the house.

On impulse, she put aside her book and jumped to her feet. She went out to the kitchen and, after rummaging through the cupboards, found the ingredients she was looking for. In a short time she had coffee percolating and was going through the refrigerator. After pouring the hot coffee into a large insulated flask, she placed that, along with several earthenware mugs and a plate of thick sandwiches, on a tray.

"I better clean up first or Myrna will shoot me for sure." Kelly laughed to herself, putting the sandwich makings back in the refrigerator and rewrapping the bread in cellophane.

The full moon lit the pathway toward the barn as Kelly walked carefully so as not to trip over any stones along the way. When she entered the large barn, she could hear men's muted voices from the other end.

"Careful, Jake; the contractions are getting stronger." Will's voice was clear and strong.

"C'mon, girl, easy, now." Jake's voice was soft and crooning, then it sharpened. "Come on, Rick, watch her! I almost got kicked in the head."

Kelly uttered an almost inaudible gasp and her hands tightened on the tray. She walked quickly down the length of the barn until she reached the end stall. She set the tray on a nearby hay bale and walked closer to see what was happening. The air was strong with the scent of men's sweaty bodies, warm horse-flesh, disinfectant, and a pungent, indefinable smell.

The three men's backs were to her as they worked together as one to help the heaving and straining mare. Jake's bare bronze back glistened with sweat from the heavy exertion of helping the mare. His muscles were tight cords from the strain he was placing on them.

"All right, he's coming." Even his voice was tight with strain and weariness. "Not much longer now, old girl," Jake soothed the heaving mare. "Pretty soon you'll be able to see your new baby."

This was a new experience for Kelly, who had always been a city girl. Even when she had visited her brother's horse farm she had never witnessed the birth process. She watched the chestnut-colored mare heave to be rid of her unwieldy burden, and it was not long before a slick bundle slid onto the straw-covered floor. The mare turned her head to nuzzle the foal's neck as she nickered softly to her child and began to lick him dry.

"A colt, Jake," Will said proudly. "A fine-looking colt. He'll do us proud; I can tell already."

"Yeah." Jake straightened up tiredly. As he turned, his surprised eyes fell on the silent Kelly.

"I—ah—I made some coffee and sandwiches," she said lamely, gesturing toward the tray. "I thought you might like something to eat."

A warmth that Kelly had never seen before crept into Jake's eyes. "Thank you, Kelly," he said quietly.

Swiftly turning to hide the flush stealing up her cheeks, Kelly began to pour the coffee into the mugs.

"We sure appreciate this, Kelly." Will grinned, munching on one of the sandwiches.

"Ever seen a foaling before?" Jake asked in a low voice.

"No." Her honey-colored hair slid forward to hide her flushed cheeks as she shook her head.

"This might help get rid of some of the jitters you probably feel right now." He handed Kelly his coffee mug.

Accepting the mug, she made sure not to drink from the same side as Jake. Seeing her action, he grinned as he shrugged his shirt back on, leaving it unbuttoned and hanging loose. Keeping his eyes on Kelly's flushed face, Jake deliberately turned the cup to drink from the same side she had just drunk from. His emerald eyes danced with wicked lights as he saw Kelly's stricken expression.

"Jake!" Kelly whispered. "They'll see you."

"In case you haven't noticed, we're alone." His amused whisper brought a deeper flush to her cheeks as she quickly looked around to find that Will and Rick had gone. They had left without her noticing it. "I guess they wanted the new mother to have some time alone with her son."

Kelly looked down at the spindly-legged colt, who had finally managed to stand up and walk with faltering steps to his mother. Tears sprang to her eyes as she gazed on this new life that Jake had helped bring into the world. Unable to speak, Kelly looked up at Jake, her eyes shimmering like two jewels. Jake's eyes darkened on seeing the expression on her face.

"You're a romantic at heart, Kelly James," he said huskily. "I think there are times when you prefer to hide it, but you're not very good at it."

"You, Jake Cassidy, have kissed the Blarney Stone too many times," Kelly smilingly retorted.

"That isn't what I've been wanting to kiss." She barely had time to take in the meaning of Jake's words before he pulled her into his arms and his mouth descended on hers in a searing kiss. Kelly couldn't have protested if she had wanted to. And she certainly didn't want to. Her mouth parted under his probing touch, allowing him to deepen the kiss. Kelly's arms encircled Jake's neck as she pressed herself against his warm, sweaty body.

"I'm filthy and I need a shower." Jake turned his head in order to let his lips and teeth explore the sensitive skin near Kelly's ear. "Care to join me?"

Kelly's body stiffened in shock as she abruptly drew away from his embrace. Jake laughed at the outraged expression on her face.

"You're a joy to tease." He dropped a kiss on her nose as he slid an arm around her waist, pulling her against his side. "Leave the tray. I'm bone-tired and want my rest. You can help me up to the house."

As they walked with their arms around each other's waist, Kelly felt happier than she had in a long time. She didn't know why Jake had decided to stop being mad at her, but she wasn't going to complain. She giggled as Jake growled teasing and wicked comments into her ear as they went slowly up to the house. Every few steps he would stop, pulling her into his embrace for a hard and searching kiss. Inside the house, Jake still refused to relinquish his grip on her waist.

"The least I can do is see the lady to her door," he gallantly informed Kelly. "You can never be too sure what roguish man could be lurking about."

In front of her bedroom door, Kelly leaned back against the wood, smiling up at him, barely able to make out his strong features in the dim light.

"Thank you again for the coffee and sandwiches," Jake said softly, resting one hand on the door near Kelly's left shoulder.

"I'm glad I thought of it." She slid her arms around his bare waist and reached up, pressing a kiss against his lips. Unable to remain immune to the soft body moving against his, Jake tightened his arms to bring Kelly back to him for another searing kiss. When he finally released her, his breathing was ragged and labored.

"Dream of me, Kelly James." Jake's voice was husky as he rested a finger against her lips. Then he turned to stride away down the hall.

Kelly opened her bedroom door and slipped inside. As she washed her face and then undressed, the smile never left her face, until a sobering thought struck her. Jake was more than interested in her. There was no doubt of that. But which person was he interested in? Kelly James, the beautiful and successful fashion model, who was also very desirable to members of the opposite sex? Or Kelly James, the woman, who wanted a man to want her for herself, not her fame? For something longer lasting than just the physical desire that wouldn't last into the future when people grew old and gray. For once, she regretted the beauty she had been blessed with.

The next morning, Kelly sighed inwardly on viewing the large breakfast Myrna set before her.

"Every bit, now," the cook reminded her, adding, "You going down to watch the horse-breaking?"

"Horsebreaking?" She looked up.

"Jake and some of the men are going to start breaking saddle horses this morning." Myrna returned to the kitchen and called back over her shoulder, "There's going to be a lot of bruises and perhaps some broken bones by this evening, if not sooner."

Kelly looked down at her eggs and bacon, her appetite now entirely gone. She didn't want to go down to the corral to watch men being thrown off bucking horses, but she couldn't bear to stay away, either. After she forced down the last bite of her breakfast, Kelly hurried to her bedroom to change from her sandals to boots.

As she walked down to the corrals Kelly could hear the men's shouts from some distance away. Inside the largest corral, two men were holding the bridle of a snorting buckskin whose rolling eyes displayed his distress. One man stood nearby, ready to mount. The rest of the men stood outside the corral, calling out encouragement to their co-worker.

Kelly approached the corral and sought out Will. The older man grinned at her. "Come to see Jake ride a bronc?"

"I'm not too sure," she confessed, her eyes darting around to look for the tall, rugged figure. She soon found her objective. Across the corral, Jake's eyes met hers, his crinkling in the bright sunshine.

Jake looked so sure of himself as he leaned on the railing, his cigarette dangling carelessly from his mouth. His blue shirt was dusty already and the color was sure to be unrecognizable by the end of the day. His brown hat was pulled forward, shading his bronzed face.

Kelly shoved her hands into the pockets of

her jeans so that she wouldn't keep clasping them nervously in front of her. The man who had been preparing to mount the skittish buckskin slowly climbed into the saddle, picking up the reins and nodding to the men holding the horse's head. They released their hold and hurriedly backed off. The buckskin wheeled around, then began bucking, trying to throw off the unfamiliar weight on his back. It didn't take him long to dispose of his rider. Amid hoots and catcalls, the disgruntled man slapped at the seat of his jeans.

"There must be an easier way," Kelly said in an alarmed voice.

"No one's found it yet," Will told her.

As the morning passed, Kelly watched the men get repeatedly bucked off various horses. There were times when she held her breath, afraid the rider would be crushed against the fence. Finally, deciding that she had seen enough, Kelly turned to return to the house as Will's voice stopped her.

"Looks like Jake's going to ride that bay, after all."

"No!" she whispered in an agitated tone, looking in Jake's direction. After talking to one of his men, he flipped his cigarette away and entered the corral with an unhurried stride. "Oh, Will, he'll get hurt!" She gripped the older man's arm.

"No, he'll be just fine," he reassured her, patting her shoulder in a kindly gesture.

Kelly's eyes were glued to the tall man talking softly to the restive horse as he slowly swung himself up into the saddle. It was a scene more dramatic than any she had seen on television. The horse wheeled and bucked frantically. She wanted to shut her eyes, yet she was afraid to. The horse finally crashed into the corral fence, unseating Jake. He was momentarily still as the men ran over to him, helping him to his feet.

Kelly could feel the nausea rising in her stomach. Afraid she would be sick, she covered her mouth with her hand and ran to the barn, breathing deeply to dispel the sick feeling. Thoughts of Jake's broken body lying on the ground only increased her agitation. She gasped back a sob as a pair of arms curled around her waist, pulling her back against a hard chest.

"Are you all right?" Jake asked quietly. "You were looking pretty green out there."

"You-you could have been killed!" Kelly sobbed. "How could you do such a thing? Are you all right?"

"I'm fine. I knew that bloody horse would try a stunt like that." He turned her around in his arms.

"All I could see was you lying there hurt like your father!" she cried out. "How can you do something so dangerous? So crazy? So—" Her tearful tirade was cut off by the swift descent of Jake's mouth to hers. Kelly's tears mingled with their kiss, giving it a salty taste.

Jake's hands roamed down over her body, arching her that much more fully against him. When he finally released her, her sobs had been reduced to ragged gasps.

"You were starting to get hysterical," Jake

told her calmly. "It was the best way to stop you."

"You mean instead of your other method?" she asked quietly.

Jake took a handkerchief out of his jeans pocket and dabbed at Kelly's tears, then had her blow her nose. He pressed her cheek against his chest, stroking her hair in a soothing gesture.

"I don't intend to break anything, honey," he murmured in her ear. "If anything, I was probably showing off some, knowing you were there watching me. Like some crazy kid. Am I forgiven?"

Kelly looked up, unable to be angry or upset when Jake looked so sensually appealing. She rubbed her cheek against the soft cloth of his shirt, like a kitten seeking affection.

"I was so afraid you'd get hurt, " she mumbled. "Or break something."

"Let's go up to the house, and I'll shock Myrna by staying for lunch." Jake kept his arm around her shoulders as they walked out of the barn. Calling out to his men, he kept pace with Kelly's slower steps as they walked up the pathway.

"There has to be an easier way to break horses," Kelly persisted as they approached the house.

"Well, if one comes along, you can be assured that I'll be the first to try it out." He grinned. "I'm starting to get too old for all this."

Chapter Six

Kelly stood before the old-fashioned looking glass in Maureen's sitting room, staring at her reflection in fascination.

"I never thought that was the right color for me, but on you it's just lovely," Maureen said confidently.

"I don't feel as if I'm looking at *me*." Kelly laughed, twirling around and feeling the graceful folds swirl around her ankles.

"Now, stand still so I don't stick any pins in you," Myrna ordered. "We want this gown finished in time. And we can't do that if you insist on running around admiring yourself," she joked.

The gown was of cornflower-blue satin, with paler blue velvet ribbon trim. The low, rounded neckline accented her high breasts and creamy shoulders, and the tiny sleeves left her arms bare. The full skirt fell gracefully to her feet.

"Curl her hair up and string ribbons through the curls, and she'll look as if she just stepped out of a picture," Maureen told Myrna as if Kelly weren't even there. "We'll need to take the waist in a little and let out the bust. She'll be the belle of the ball. She'll have every man under the age of ninety begging her for a dance."

I only care about one man's opinion, Kelly thought to herself as she dutifully turned when Myrna or Maureen told her to.

"Tomorrow's the race," Myrna commented. "Jake will win, if he doesn't break anything first."

"Myrna," Maureen reproved. "That only happened because Rob Carlson's horse ran into his. Now, do be careful; you're frightening Kelly."

"I guess I never thought of a horse race as being dangerous," Kelly confessed. "I just thought of a bunch of horses running around a track to see who would finish first."

"Jake is an excellent horseman and he'll be out there to win, not to take chances," Maureen reassured her. "Because of his father's accident he has never taken any unnecessary chances. Now, please stand very still as we take the dress off so the pins won't stick you."

Kelly sighed, unsure if she wanted to watch the horse race after all. Jake had demanded her promise that she would be sure to attend to cheer him on to the finish line. Now she was afraid she would be there to see him carried off the field on a stretcher. It wasn't until after dinner that she could voice her fears to him. They had walked out onto the porch, where Jake stretched out on a lounge chair and Kelly ensconced herself in his lap.

She no longer cared which Kelly James Jake was interested in; she was just happy that he was interested in her at all.

"They said you could be hurt tomorrow," she murmured, resting her cheek in the hollow of his shoulder. "That you've been hurt before."

"Not to worry, hon," he consoled her. "I haven't had such a lovely cheering section before. I'm certainly not going to tumble off my horse unless you promise to be there to nurse me back to health."

"It isn't funny, Jake," Kelly cried out, turning her head to look up at him. "After what happened to your father—" Her words were silenced by the hard, unyielding pressure of Jake's mouth on hers.

"*Nothing* will happen to me." His voice was harsh and rough. "Because I won't allow anything to happen to me. Not now," he finished cryptically.

Kelly's forefinger traced the outline of Jake's lips. They opened slightly and he took her finger between his strong teeth, lightly biting the skin.

"You're taking all of my fears, bundling them up, and tossing them away," she said softly. "But they'll just come back when you're not there. I don't want you to get hurt. Who will I have to dance with if you're laid up with a broken leg or something?" she teased.

"I'd make you stay home and be my nurse," he arrogantly told her, a hand sliding possessively along her hip. "Now, why don't you just shut up and let me kiss you like I've been wanting to do since dinner."

Smiling, Kelly lifted her face for Jake's kiss. Her arms moved around his neck and she shifted her position slightly in his lap.

"Stop it," Jake said thickly. "Or be prepared to make love right out here."

"Your mother," she murmured in protest.

"Forget my mother." His hard mouth effectively stopped any further conversation.

The following day, Kelly was by Maureen's side at the large grounds set aside for local horse shows, races, and fairs.

"Patrick and Susan, his wife, will be coming down this afternoon for the gala." Maureen spoke of her younger son with pride.

"Is he like Jake?" Kelly's eyes were on the tall, black-haired figure seated on the black stallion who was restively pawing the ground, impatient to run.

"Patrick?" She smiled fondly. "He and Jake are as different as night and day. Patrick has a gentle nature, and I've yet to see him lose his temper. He and Susan are perfectly matched. She's a lovely girl who takes care of his home and their two children without any fuss. You'll see what I mean when they arrive."

Kelly had worn brown cords with an apricot silk shirt, and a brown-and-apricot print scarf held her hair away from her face. The earth tones suited her golden coloring, giving her a warm look. When she and Maureen walked past Sheila, the auburn-haired woman gazed freezingly at her.

"You'd better be ready to congratulate the winner." They turned at the sound of Jake's voice. His eyes were focused on Kelly's up-turned face.

"You sound confident that you'll win," she said, feeling nervous twinges in her stomach at the blatant sensuality in Jake's eyes.

Without answering, Jake leaned down from the saddle and pulled the scarf from Kelly's hair. She gave a cry of dismay and her hand flew up to her tumbled hair.

"The lady always gives her knight a token before he goes into battle," Jake murmured, casually tying the scarf around his neck. "I'll collect my kiss after the race."

Maureen, who had moved away from the interchange, now stepped forward to touch Kelly's arm. "We better get to our seats."

Kelly looked back up at Jake, the expression on her face saying more than words could. She didn't want to see him hurt.

"My good-luck talisman." He grinned, touching the scarf at his throat. "I don't in-tend to get it dirty for you." Touching his heels to the flanks of his mount, he rode off as the loudspeaker blared out a request for the riders to line up.

As Kelly and Maureen took their seats, which were uncomfortably near Sheila, the other woman's eyes fell on Kelly's tousled hair. Then she looked across the course to see the scarf now knotted casually around Jake's bronzed throat.

"I have an idea that Sheila is quite unhappy," Maureen murmured in Kelly's ear.

"I don't know why she's worrying." Kelly gave a short laugh. "After all, I'll be leaving for New York soon and she'll have Jake all to herself again."

Maureen gave Kelly a questioning look but said nothing. She turned to face the course as the announcer read off the names of the riders.

Kelly jumped at the sound of the starting gun. Her eyes were on one rider only. He was not difficult to spot as he sat the huge black horse who ran with the quickness of the wind. At one point another horse seemed to bump into Banshee, almost throwing him off balance. Kelly gasped in horror, closing her eyes tightly, unwilling to watch the horse fall and the rider be pitched to the ground.

"He's all right, Kelly." Maureen's voice was controlled but full of excitement.

Kelly's turquoise eyes flew open as the huge stallion sped past the finish line.

"Jake won!" Kelly squealed, grabbing Maureen's arm. "He won!"

"We'd better get down to him." Maureen's face shone with pride in her son as she rose to her feet.

As soon as Jake dismounted he was surrounded by well-wishers. But his eyes moved everywhere, as if he were looking for someone special. When he saw Kelly coming, with Maureen following at a slower pace, his eyes lit up.

Suddenly Sheila darted in front. "Congratulations, darling," she said throatily, slipping her arms around Jake's neck and pulling his face down for her kiss.

Kelly halted in her tracks. Narrowing her eyes, she marched determinedly toward the couple. When Sheila finally released Jake, he looked up to see Kelly's set features. A glint of amusement danced in the emerald depths of his eyes. Following his gaze, Sheila turned to smile icily at Kelly.

"She wants to make you jealous," Maureen whispered in Kelly's ear.

"Oh, does she?" Kelly muttered. "I'll give *her* something to think about, instead."

Kelly walked forward until she stood in front of Jake. Smiling up at his wary face, she slid her arms around his neck. "For my gallant knight," she murmured before pressing her lips against his.

The crowd around them broke into jokes and loud laughter as Kelly pressed herself close to Jake's hard body. His hands curled around her waist. Feeling suddenly embarrassed by her forward action, Kelly tried to draw back, but Jake's arms tightened, refusing to allow her to escape his embrace.

"You started it, you can finish it," Jake murmured against Kelly's lips. Finally releasing her, he looked up, grinning at his friends. "Better than any trophy." He kept an arm casually draped over Kelly's shoulders, his eyes meeting his mother's in silent communication. "If you want to go back now to get things ready for Pat, Kelly can ride with me. I want to do some celebrating first."

Nodding, Maureen turned to walk back in the direction of the car.

"What if I didn't want to stay behind with you?" Kelly looked up, arching an eyebrow.

"I'm the champion, Kelly." The one sentence said it all as far as he was concerned.

Keeping Kelly close to his side, he held the reins in his other hand and began walking, still laughing and joking with his friends.

"Where are we going?" Kelly asked curiously.

"First I'm handing Banshee over to Will to be trucked back to the station; then I'm taking you over to the pub for some drinks," Jake replied, not slowing his stride.

After arranging to meet his friends at the local pub, Jake and Kelly walked over to a large horse van. Will was standing in front, smiling widely.

"You showed 'em again, boy." The elderly man slapped Jake on the back. "Just like your pa afore you. That was one fine race you rode."

"I tried my best," Jake replied. "Kelly and I are going over to the pub to celebrate. We'll be home in time for dinner, though." Then Jake led Kelly toward a station wagon, helping her inside.

The drive to the pub was short and quiet, but this time the silence was a companionable one. Jake stopped the car in front of the pub. After getting out of the car, he walked around to hold the passenger door open for Kelly. He stood close, so that she was only inches from him when she stepped out. Looking down at her upturned face, Jake slowly untied the scarf from around his neck and slid it off, draping it around Kelly's. Pulling both ends of the soft silk material, he drew her face up for a kiss. Her arms slid around his waist, and she pressed herself against him, letting the heat from his body warm hers.

"Much better," Jake said huskily. "We'll continue this later in a more appropriate setting."

"Sure of yourself, aren't you?" Kelly asked provocatively.

"You know it."

Inside the pub, Jake was greeted all around by congratulatory friends. A number of them directed curious and admiring glances at the beautiful honey-blond woman at his side as he led Kelly toward the rear of the room. He found a table and sat her down before heading for the bar to get their drinks. As she watched him cross the room Kelly could see how popular he was with the local ranchers.

Jake was soon back with their drinks; he placed a glass of white wine in front of Kelly and then set down his own glass. He sat down on the bench beside her, his thigh brushing lightly against hers and one arm draped along the back of the bench against her shoulders.

"To the winner," Kelly said softly, raising her glass in a toast.

Jake's eyes gazed intently into hers as they drank.

"What are you drinking?" she asked curiously.

"Stout."

Kelly looked confused as she studied Jake's foaming glass.

"It's an extremely strong form of beer," he explained with a grin, picking up his glass and handing it to Kelly. "Want to try some?"

Kelly accepted the glass and took a cautious sip. As the strong alcohol burned a path down her throat, her eyes stung and she couldn't stop herself from coughing. Laughing, Jake slapped her on the back.

"A bit strong for you?"

"I—it's not funny." Kelly choked, groping for her wineglass. "Why didn't you warn me?"

"Because it's nice to have you at a disadvantage every once in a while," he said in the low voice that was so seductive to Kelly's senses.

Jake lifted her hand, palm up, to press his lips against her sensitive skin, teasing it with his tongue and teeth. He glanced up, noting the heated flush rising in Kelly's cheeks.

"How touching!"

Taking his time, Jake slowly put Kelly's hand down, although he kept a tight hold on it and would not allow her to draw away. His eyes were icy emeralds when he finally lifted them to an angry Sheila who was standing before them.

"I realize that you have to be polite to your guest, darling," Sheila drawled. "But I do hope that doesn't mean making love to her in public."

Kelly's muscles tensed when she saw the intimate expression Sheila directed at Jake. Sensing her discomfort, Jake reassuringly squeezed her hand.

"There hasn't been anything between you and me for a long time now, Sheila," Jake said flatly. "Don't try to make something out of nothing."

Sheila's eyes narrowed in fury as she turned to Kelly. "You may have Jake now, but no one has ever been able to keep him for long. He'll soon tire of you and you'll lose him, just like the others did." Sheila spun around and stalked out of the pub.

"I'm sorry." Jake turned to Kelly with a heavy sigh. "I didn't think she'd make a scene. If I had, I wouldn't have brought you here."

"Sheila's in love with you," she said softly. "She's hurt, so all she can do is lash out."

"Sheila is only in love with Sheila," he said harshly. "I was handy to have nearby, that's all. She never lacks for men."

Kelly silently digested Jake's words as she finished her wine.

"We'd better start back to the house." Jake glanced down at his watch. "Pat is due to arrive anytime, and Myrna will have my hide if we're late for dinner."

Once in the car, Jake half turned in his seat and pulled Kelly into his arms for a hard kiss; he released her only reluctantly.

"I could still turn you over my knee for not telling me that pretty boy is your brother," he muttered against her neck, nibbling the sensitive skin. "Um, you taste good."

"Jake!" Kelly protested laughingly as she playfully pushed him away. "Your mother is going to wonder what's happened to us."

"O.K., I get the message." Jake grinned, the warmth softening his harsh features. He turned back to switch on the ignition. "Just sit within touching distance."

Kelly obediently slid across the seat until she sat close to Jake. Later, when he had turned off the main road onto the road leading to the house, an imp of mischief prompted Kelly to turn in her seat, curl her legs up underneath her, and rest her crossed arms on Jake's shoulder. With her forefinger she carefully traced the outline of his ear in a slow, sensual motion. Shuddering, he reached up and gripped her wrist.

"Stop it, Kelly; do you want us to have a wreck?" he demanded thickly. "I'm not made of stone."

"You're not exactly handsome, you know," she commented idly, as if Jake hadn't spoken. "Rugged-looking, that's a good description. Or even craggy. You have an interesting face."

"Thanks for the compliment," he said dryly.

"Oh, Jake." Kelly's voice came out in a soft sigh. "Why were you so horrible to me before? All we did was insult each other, and now . . ."

"And now, all we want to do is make love to each other," he finished softly. "I've discovered that I was wrong about a lot of things concerning you, and I've also discovered that I can't keep my hands off you. You're not some vain model who's always worrying about her figure or her looks. You're just as beautiful when you're all wet and coming out of the pool with your hair slicked back and no makeup on as you are right now, with your hair all soft and curly."

Jake stopped the car in front of the house and turned off the engine. He turned in his seat to face Kelly, his palms framing her face.

"You're just the way I want you," he said quietly. "But we have quite a few misunderstandings to clear up soon. There are so many things I want to say, and I'm not too sure where to begin." Suddenly he was interrupted by a man's laughing shout from the front door and the sudden bright glare of the porch light being switched on.

"Hey, big brother, I thought you'd be too old to be caught necking in the car. Bring your lady in so we can meet her. From what I hear, she isn't half bad."

Kelly couldn't help but giggle when she heard what Jake was muttering under his breath.

"Brother Pat has arrived with his gang." Jake got out of the car and helped Kelly slide out after him. As they climbed the steps to the front door Jake's hand rested possessively at the small of her back, steering her inside.

Inside the brightly lit house they were surrounded by the rest of the Cassidy family. Kelly liked Pat at once. Thirty-two years old to Jake's thirty-six, Pat had the same gleaming black hair, but his eyes were a lighter shade of green and not as intense. It was obvious that he often wore a happy smile and probably never lost his temper. One look at Susan told Kelly that he'd found the perfect wife, one whose short brown curls and bouncy personality perfectly complemented her tall, good-looking husband. Tugging at Maureen's skirts were two small children, a little boy of six, named Billy, and a little girl of four, called Sally; both were the image of their father.

"Kelly, lass, where were you ten years ago?" Pat gave a mock sigh, earning him a playful punch in the ribs from his wife.

"In junior high school in the United States," Kelly replied, grinning.

"A mere child." He shook his head as he draped an arm about his brother's shoulders. "I do admit that your taste is improving, Jake. This one looks passable."

"Thanks," Jake growled.

"Don't mind Pat." Susan took Kelly aside. "He's always been a tease, and he really enjoys getting Jake's goat. Those two have been at it for years."

"My brother and I are the same," she assured her.

"I'm going to put the children to bed while you all get acquainted." Maureen came up behind them, holding a sleepy Sally in her arms. "Myrna said dinner won't be ready for another half hour still."

Wide-eyed, Sally studied Kelly from beneath long black lashes. She held out pudgy fingers toward Kelly's hair.

"Pwetty," Sally mumbled. "Like my dolly." Kelly smiled warmly, unable to resist the little girl's charm.

"Blond hair on a live person is a novelty to her," Susan explained.

"She's adorable," Kelly said honestly. "I'd love a dozen just like her. You must be very proud of both of them." Since her back was to Jake, she didn't see the probing look he flashed her.

"That's because they're acting like angels for Grandma." Susan laughed. "They both take after their father and never run down. They're actually a full-time job, but I wouldn't trade them for anything. Maureen said that you're a model in New York. You must love it."

The two young women chatted as the two brothers stood next to the bar, arguing good-naturedly.

"Jake's something else, isn't he?" Susan commented, seeing the direction of Kelly's gaze. "I can remember when I was in school; all the girls had a crush on him. I became very popular with them since I was dating his brother. But Jake was always very selective about whom he dated. Of course, managing the station didn't give him a lot of free time to date. He had too many responsibilities around here, instead. He's not an easy man to know or understand, but he's one of the best ones around."

"This sounds like a bit of matchmaking," Kelly replied. "Obviously Maureen neglected to inform you that I'll be leaving for New York City in a week or so. My brother and I have some business details to settle."

Susan smiled confidently. "Then you don't know Jake very well, do you? He doesn't give up easily."

"Neither do I."

Further conversation was halted by Myrna's announcement that dinner was ready.

"And none of that whiskey on my table," she told Jake and Pat in a tart voice. "I won't have my beautiful meal ruined by hard liquor."

"Ah, I've missed you, beautiful." Pat kissed the cook's cheek. "If it wasn't for my wife and that husband of yours, I'd spirit you away this minute," he added in a mock whisper.

Dinner that evening was livelier than usual with Pat and Susan to add their own brand of fun to the situation. Eventually the two men settled down to talking over events surrounding the station and the daily problems that cropped up. Now, seeing Pat's serious side, Kelly could see the similarity between the two brothers. There was no question, though, as to who was in charge of the vast lands. Jake was aware and in control of everything that went on, even in areas that he didn't see every day.

Maureen protested when she overheard the men talking about going down to the barn to see the new foal after dinner.

"You can do that tomorrow," she said firmly. "I don't get to have all of my family around me very often, so I intend to take full advantage this evening. We women will be busy tomorrow preparing for the gala in the evening. Then you two can go through the barns as much as you please, as long as you're ready on time."

For the balance of the evening Jake appeared edgy and his eyes kept drifting toward Kelly. Once she looked up at him, but on seeing the blatant sensuality in his gaze she had to lower her eyes as she felt the heat rise in her body. It was obvious that he would have preferred that they be alone this evening, but he could hardly be rude to his family. Several times Pat noticed the exchange of glances between his brother and Kelly and a slight smile curved his lips. Susan, too, was not unaware of the current flowing between the two of them. An unspoken communication passed between husband and wife.

"Well, it was a long drive out here." Pat stood up and stretched tiredly. "Coming, Sue?" He turned to his wife.

She nodded and rose to her feet, as well. Maureen had retired earlier so as to be fresh for the following day.

"See you in the morning, Jake, Kelly." Pat and Susan walked down the hallway to their room, leaving Kelly and Jake alone in the den.

Kelly sat uneasily in her chair as Jake walked over to the bar and splashed whiskey into his glass. Then he pulled Kelly out of her chair and sat down in it himself, drawing her down onto his lap.

"This is much better," he murmured in her ear, setting his glass down on the nearby table.

"You practically drove them out of here," Kelly accused him. "What can they think of us?"

"That we prefer to be alone." Jake's hand curved around Kelly's hip, then moved upward in a caressing motion. "I don't want to share you with anyone right now. Besides, they're married. They can find something to do," he said wickedly.

"Why can't I stay angry with you?" She smiled, pushing the unruly hair away from his forehead, loving the intimate gesture. "There are times you're so arrogant that I *should* stand there and scream horrible things at you, but I don't want to."

"Because there are more pleasurable ways to spend our time." His finger traced the neckline of Kelly's shirt down to the deep V, casually unbuttoning the top button, then the next.

"Jake!" Her face burned with embarrassment. "Someone could come in."

"You've been living a life where you probably think nothing of undressing in front of photographers, yet you seem so shy of showing off your beautiful body," he mused.

"I don't make a habit of undressing in front of anyone," Kelly said sharply. "We've always been given dressing rooms and all the privacy we want. Why can't you understand that I'm not that type of person? Very few models that I know are like that."

"Every time I think I'm beginning to understand you, you surprise me with a new side of yourself." Jake's finger traced the contours of Kelly's face, as if memorizing them. "You certainly don't make it easy for a man."

"It didn't seem like you wanted to understand me the first time you met me," she informed him.

"When you walked into that room, I thought

you were the most beautiful woman I had ever seen," he said quietly.

"And I thought you were rude, arrogant, and the most exasperating man I had ever met." Kelly's arms crept around Jake's neck.

"At least I'm consistent."

"Don't tease, Jake," she pleaded, resting her head in the hollow of his shoulder. "For the first time in weeks we're talking without arguing or insulting each other. Let's enjoy this."

"Now, that is an idea I'll gladly go along with." Jake bent his head, moving his lips along hers in a light, teasing motion. As Kelly responded his kiss deepened, his lips parting hers to further explore, taste, and savor. Her arms tightened as if refusing to let him go.

"No more," Jake muttered thickly, lifting his head. "I'm at the breaking point now." His hand pressed her cheek against his shoulder as he rested his chin on the top of her head. It was several moments before the two of them were able to breathe normally.

Kelly closed her eyes, content just to have Jake's arms around her in this warm embrace.

"What will you do when you get back to New York?" Jake's quiet voice startled her out of her reverie.

All of a sudden, reality came back in a cold rush. It wouldn't be long before she would have to leave Australia—and Jake.

"Kyle's and my contracts are up for renewal soon," Kelly said in a small voice. "Of course, it's only a formality."

"And when Pegasus decides they want a new image? What will you do then? Your brother has his writing career to fall back on. What will you have?"

Kelly could feel the tension in Jake's body as he waited for her answer. Would it matter to him? Would it really matter what happened to her? "I don't know," she said honestly. "Some models become cosmetics or fashion consultants for well-known companies. Some teach at modeling schools; some retire, marry, and have a family." Her voice dropped. "Others continue their careers for many years. So how can I say what I'll do a few years from now?" *I want to stay here with you!* her mind cried out to him. *Don't let me leave!*

As if sensing Kelly's inner qualms, although not understanding them, Jake's arms tightened around her. "I'm sure you miss the bright city lights," he said finally, but the harshness with which he usually said such things was gone from his voice.

Desperate not to reveal any of her feelings for him by answering honestly, Kelly merely stayed silent, not realizing that Jake might take that to mean yes. Instead, she just burrowed her face deeper against his shoulder, gratefully accepting his silent comfort.

It was much later that Kelly retired to her room for bed. Lying against the cool sheets, she thought back over the changes that had come over Jake and herself in the past few days.

Kelly had no doubt that Sheila hated her, but Jake's indifference toward the other woman had surprised Kelly. She hadn't realized that he no longer cared at all for Sheila. Of course, Kelly was aware that all that could change after she returned to New York. Her face grew pensive at the heart-wrenching thought of leaving this peaceful existence for the frantic pace of that other world. It was a world that didn't seem real to her anymore. This was what seemed real. The scent of exotic blossoms wafting through the air into her bedroom, learning needlepoint from Maureen, going for rides with Will and Jake, feeling a part of this warm household. Kelly had never before known anyone like Maureen, who could make a guest feel part of the family. She had grown to be very fond of the older woman, and even fonder of her son. The word *love* drifted through Kelly's mind, but the word was one that she had rejected so often in the past that she was afraid to believe that that was what she felt for Jake, not just physical attraction. She was already aware of how much Jake wanted her in the physical sense, and that she wanted him just as deeply, but she knew now that she wanted much more from this man than that.

Kelly knew she should be making plans to return to the States soon, but she felt hesitant. She didn't want to return to the noise, the hectic schedules, the photo sessions, the men who only saw her as a beautiful face, the empty life without meaning or purpose. Jake had spoiled her by seeing beneath the makeup and carefully styled hair. How could she return to that life now after seeing a more meaningful life here?

She thought of the love and warmth that were so evident between Pat and Susan. The younger Cassidy brother had never been far from his wife's side that evening, holding her hand or keeping an arm draped around her shoulders. Kelly envied them their love for each other and their children. Sighing, she curled up under the covers and closed her eyes to sleep.

Chapter Seven

The following day was chaotic for all three women. Jake and Pat took Billy and Sally with them to the barns and swimming to keep the children from being underfoot while the women got dressed for the gala.

"Every year we go through the same thing," Pat told his brother. "They take all day to look beautiful for one evening. Then we have to spend the entire time assuring them that they look all right because they're afraid they either overdid it or didn't do enough. We can't win, either way."

"They don't intend us to," Jake replied.

Kelly enjoyed her leisurely bubble bath, relaxing in the warm water with her freshly set hair bound up in a towel. After her bath, she manicured her nails and polished them in a pale rose shade.

With Maureen's help, Kelly's honey-gold tresses were pulled back in loose curls with pale blue velvet ribbons threaded through them. Luminescent pearl stud earrings drew attention to her delicate ears. Kelly kept her makeup to a minimum, using only a light touch of smoky blue eye shadow and the barest sweep of blusher across her cheekbones. Her lip gloss was a deep rose shade.

"How is it that you can wear makeup yet look as if you aren't wearing any at all?" Susan asked later when Kelly had gone to see how she was getting along. "You look absolutely beautiful."

"It takes more time to get the unmade-up look," Kelly told her, eyeing Susan's elfin features with a keen eye. "I'd really like to try to accent your eyes more, if you'd let me. They're your best feature and should be played up."

"Please do," Susan said breathlessly. "Every time I try to wear more than lipstick, I look like a little girl caught playing with her mother's makeup."

"Wait a minute and let me get my cosmetics bag." Kelly hurried to her bedroom and returned with the suede bag. Rummaging through several cases of eye shadow, Kelly finally selected a smoky bronze shade with gold highlights.

Susan sat still as Kelly worked quickly but deftly, using a brown mascara to complement the eye shadow. She finished with a dusting of tawny blusher.

"Now you can look," Kelly said crisply, stepping back to allow Susan to look in the dressing-table mirror.

Susan studied her reflection in the mirror, unable to believe what she saw. Her hazel eyes appeared greener, with golden lights dancing in their depths, while her usual elfin features had been transformed into a delicate cameo effect.

"That's me?" Susan whispered in awe.

"Of course," Kelly replied with a warm smile.

"You're a magician."

"No, I'm not." Kelly shook her head, still smiling. "All I did was highlight your best features to bring them out."

"Could you teach me how to do all this?" Susan asked. "And tell me what to buy? I certainly don't want to lose this new me now that I've found her."

"It's very easy to do. And to be honest, these shades look much better on you than they did on me. I have a horrible habit of going on a makeup binge every once in a while and buying everything in sight."

A mischievous grin curved Susan's lips. "I have an idea that the new me is going to throw Pat for a loop, but that he'll like her very much."

"Men deserve to be thrown off balance every once in a while. They always think they can get the best of us. Little do they know it's actually the other way around." Kelly laughed, wishing she felt as confident as she sounded.

After leaving Susan, Kelly went back to her room. Looking through her suitcase, she came upon the manila envelope her father had given her. She sat on the edge of the bed, holding the envelope in her lap. Finally making up her mind, she slipped on a robe and headed for Maureen's room; she knew that the older woman would be resting at this hour. She knocked and, after being bidden to enter, she opened the door. Maureen looked up with a smile from her chintz-covered chaise.

"Maureen." Kelly hesitated, then the words rushed out in a torrent. "My father gave me this. It—it holds a picture of you and him and the letters you had written him while he was in the hospital. Daddy had wanted you to have these. I hope you don't mind that I read the letters. They were beautiful." She handed Maureen the envelope.

The older woman looked down, slowly turning the envelope over in her hands. "I don't mind at all," she said softly.

"Actually, it was those letters that convinced me I should come here to see you," Kelly said quietly. "They were so warm, so full of love. I wanted to meet the woman who wrote them."

"Kelly, was—was your father happy?"

"Yes, he was happy, and I know he made my mother happy. Except that she had always wanted to travel to New Zealand, and he refused to go there. Mom thought it was because of the war and never pushed the subject." She paused. "Dad wouldn't explain his reasons, and none of us ever asked."

Maureen was silent for a few moments, then looked up with a smile. "I think that it's better that Ross and I didn't get married," she said mysteriously. "I'm sure that you would agree with me."

Kelly looked at her with a confused expression on her face.

"Well, if we had, you and Jake would never

have met," Maureen pointed out with a twinkle in her eye. "Now, that wouldn't do at all, would it?"

Kelly blushed and walked toward the door. "Well, I'd better finish getting ready."

"Don't forget that the men want to leave at seven-thirty," Maureen called after her.

That evening, Kelly stood before the mirror as Susan finished fastening the last hook at the back of her dress. The gown fit her perfectly. The cornflower-blue satin fell in graceful folds to her feet, which were encased in dainty silver sandals.

"I know of one person whose dance card will be filled right away this evening," Susan told her. "The men are going to surround you like bees would a flower."

Kelly clasped the antique silver locket that Maureen had lent her around her neck. She silently wondered what Jake would think of this new Kelly James, an old-fashioned, extremely feminine Kelly.

As if she had·read Kelly's mind, Susan continued. "I have an idea that Jake's will be the name filling that card. He isn't going to want to share you with anyone. He can be very possessive."

"We're only friends, Susan," Kelly said quietly.

"Are you, Kelly? Can you think of Jake as just your friend? I've seen the way the two of you look at each other, especially the way Jake looks at you, and he doesn't care who sees him. That's something you can't hide, no matter how hard you try."

"There's nothing between us except an innocent flirtation." Kelly's protest sounded feeble even to her own ears. "I can understand that you want Jake to have what you and Pat have, but I'm not the person for him." Why did it hurt her to say that?

Susan smiled in understanding as she absently smoothed an imaginary wrinkle from the satin of her gown. "I'd think very carefully before I decided that was the way I wanted it, if I were you," she advised.

At the appointed time the two men were waiting in the living room when the three women entered. Maureen looked regal in deep mauve satin and Susan was ultrafeminine in spring green trimmed in deeper green.

Jake's face showed no emotion, although his eyes darkened to deep jade as he faced Kelly. "I think that, so the ladies' gowns don't get wrinkled, we should take two cars," he told Pat, who nodded his head in agreement while staring in fascination at his wife's new image.

Jake's dark good looks were accented by the black suit that hugged his broad shoulders and lean hips. His white ruffled shirt and satin waistcoat completed the look of a riverboat gambler. Kelly could easily picture him standing with a cigar between his teeth aboard one of the stately riverboats on the Mississippi, winning admiring glances from the women aboard, or seated confidently at the gaming tables, winning at whatever game he played.

Pat and Susan drove into town in their own car, following Jake, who took Kelly and Maureen. The large hall at the edge of town was blazing with bright lights as Jake parked the car and assisted Kelly and Maureen out. When his hand touched Kelly's, she almost jerked away; she felt as if she had been burned. Her startled eyes flew up to Jake's and she wondered if he had had the same reaction, but she could read nothing in his face.

Inside the hall, each of the women was given a small card on a silken cord meant to be looped around the wrist. When they had entered, all the men's eyes turned to the honey-blond beauty with more than casual interest. Many would have approached her if not for the dark-haired man by her side. Jake's scowl was enough to dampen even the most ardent admirer's enthusiasm.

"I want to make sure to claim one or two dances, Kelly," Pat told her, ignoring his brother's dark glare.

"I'd love you to." She smiled in return.

"That could be difficult," Jake growled, holding up Kelly's dance card for her to read. He had written his name in a bold hand completely across both sides.

"That isn't fair, Jake," Kelly said quietly, lifting her eyes to meet his in silent reproach. "To either of us."

"I don't intend to be fair when it comes to you."

"Hey, Jake!" A blond-haired man in his early thirties had decided to brave the Cassidy storm and approached the small group, his eyes on Kelly. "None of us got to meet your guest last night. You don't intend to keep her to yourself again tonight, do you?"

"Kelly James, Tim Morgan," Jake said crisply.

"I'm very pleased to meet you." Tim smiled warmly at Kelly. "I'm also hoping you'll favor me with a dance."

"Of course," she replied, stealing a sly glance at Jake's stony features.

As the music began Jake gripped Kelly's wrist. "I've already requested the first dance," he coolly informed Tim, pulling Kelly along with him toward the floor.

When they reached the dance floor, Jake drew her smoothly into his arms, their steps fitting effortlessly together.

"Why, suh, you truly are a masterful man, aren't you?" Kelly adopted a Southern-belle persona. "You purely take my breath away. I don't think you realize what you're doing to me."

Jake looked down at her face with intense eyes. "You just think about what you're doing to me."

Kelly's eyes slid away; she was all too aware of the serious undercurrents behind the light-hearted banter. She couldn't understand the emotions Jake was creating in her, and she didn't know if she wanted them. She had never seen him as intense as he was this evening. His eyes on her were the same as a physical caress, heating her blood, bringing an unknown ache to her body.

She had seen Sheila across the room, looking beautiful in bronze satin. The auburn-haired woman glanced at her indifferently, then turned away, concentrating on the man by her side. It appeared that Sheila had recovered quickly from her confrontation with Jake the previous evening, Kelly thought, returning her attention to Jake.

"Sometimes I wish you women could look like this all the time," Pat commented as he claimed Kelly for a waltz. "You look a whole lot more feminine in these dresses than in jeans and boots."

"That's because you didn't have the problem of dealing with all the paraphernalia that goes on underneath these lovely dresses," she retorted. "I'd hate to tell you how long they take to hook up."

"Ah, but the fun of unhooking them." He grinned wickedly.

"Are you sure that Susan doesn't have three children instead of two?" Kelly teased.

"She will in seven months."

Kelly looked up with a delighted smile. "Oh, Pat, how wonderful!"

"Well, she can't keep away from me." He sighed modestly. "I'm so irresistible."

"Oh, you!"

Kelly didn't lack for partners throughout the evening. The young ranchers were dismayed when she mentioned she'd be leaving in a few days, and all of them tried to persuade her to lengthen her stay. Several times she noticed Maureen either sitting or dancing with a man in his late sixties. Eventually she realized that this was the doctor who had taken care of her. When she had a chance, she asked Susan about the man.

"That's Dr. Farraday," Susan explained. "He was John's doctor all through his illness, and I have an idea he's in love with Maureen. I also think she has some feelings for him."

"Then why don't they do something about it?"

"Maureen worries about Jake the same way he worries about her. For some crazy reason, she's afraid that if she isn't around he won't be properly taken care of. That's the last thing she should worry about with Myrna there."

During the evening Kelly noticed that Jake had danced only with his mother, Susan, and herself. The rest of the time, he stood along the wall, talking with the other men. It couldn't have been for a lack of willing partners, she was certain. She had seen the admiring glances Jake had received from the women. His raw sexuality stood out, affecting every woman who came into his sphere.

"Why aren't you dancing?" Kelly asked him later. "You're an excellent dancer, so that can't be your excuse, and there's certainly an abundance of lovely women here who would just adore having you ask them for a dance."

"If I wanted to dance with one of them, I'd ask her," he said grimly.

"Well, then, Mr. Cassidy, would you consider dancing the next waltz with me?" Kelly asked demurely.

A slow smile warmed Jake's stern face. "Charmed, ma'am."

"I'll be back in a moment," she murmured.

In the powder room, Kelly smoothed her curls, freshened her lipstick, and reapplied her perfume. Then she returned to the ballroom. As she entered, her eyes wandered over the room until she saw Jake in the midst of a conversation with several other men.

"I'll get him back, you know," Sheila said in a low voice as she swept by Kelly. "You'll soon be gone and out of mind. And Jake will be back eating out of my hand."

"Be careful that he doesn't bite," Kelly said sweetly, turning away.

The men's voices stilled as she approached Jake, whose back was to her. When he turned toward her, his eyes held the same unreadable darkness as they had earlier. When the music began playing a slow, dreamy waltz, Kelly floated easily into Jake's arms and they danced as if they belonged together.

Walking out to the car hours later, Kelly smiled to herself when she noticed the full moon rising in the sky and casting a silvery light over the land. She couldn't have asked for a more romantic setting. She and Jake had left first, as Pat and Susan had been sidetracked by several friends. Maureen had stayed behind with them.

Kelly was vaguely surprised by the impersonality of Jake's touch as he assisted her into the car. "Did you enjoy the ball?" he asked her as he flicked on the ignition.

"Yes, very much," she replied, puzzled by his chilly tone.

"Good."

Kelly was even more surprised as Jake went on to discuss the various men she had danced with that evening. He went on to tell her what many of them did, since a majority had jobs in town.

After a while, Kelly became irritated by Jake's matter-of-fact voice. "I'm surprised you're not telling me who would be my best bet," Kelly said sullenly.

"You already know that," Jake said briefly, not bothering to explain further.

When they arrived back at the house, Jake parked the car along the side and they climbed the steps to the front door. As they entered the darkened house Kelly was surprised when Jake didn't immediately switch on a light. She turned toward the tall man.

"Shouldn't we—" Her voice was cut off as two strong hands gripped her arms, pulling her against a hard body as an equally hard mouth descended on her soft one.

"Do you realize what you were doing to all of those men tonight?" Jake growled in Kelly's ear after he lifted his head. "Most of them were wishing they could have you in their beds tonight."

"Even you?" she asked breathlessly.

Without replying, Jake pulled her against him again. Even in the dark, Kelly could see that his eyes glittered dangerously.

"Do you get your kicks teasing men?" he muttered thickly. "Driving them to the point of total distraction?"

Smiling, Kelly lifted her head, brushing her lips against his in a light teasing motion until his hand captured the back of her head, not allowing her to escape his deepening kiss even had she wanted to. She uttered a soft sigh of protest when Jake lifted his head.

"In another moment we're going to have company," he said huskily, rubbing his hand possessively along her hip. When he spoke again, his voice sounded harsh. "Why do you have to be so beautiful?"

"Am I, Jake? Am I beautiful?"

"If you don't get out of here right now, I'll prove to you how beautiful I think you are," he muttered in her ear.

Hearing voices on the porch, Kelly hastily smoothed her dress before hurrying down the hallway to her bedroom. Snapping on the light, she caught a glimpse of herself in the dresser mirror. Her hair had tumbled down to her shoulders, and her eyes were still glazed with emotion and her mouth swollen from Jake's passionate kisses. She was the picture of a woman who had just been thoroughly kissed and enjoyed it.

Slowly undressing, Kelly hung her gown up before slipping on a robe and going into the bathroom. She wrapped a towel around her hair before she stood under the shower, allowing the water to cool her heated blood. After her shower, Kelly brushed out her hair and carefully cleaned her face. Then she slipped on a pale coral cotton nightgown.

Kelly found it impossible to sleep, with Jake's actions still crowding her mind. She finally threw back the bedcovers and got up, walking out onto the veranda. Breathing in the exotic scents of the surrounding eucalyptus blossoms, Kelly rested her folded arms on the railing and looked out into the night.

A smile curved her lips as she thought about Jake. She remembered the times he had been angry with her, the times he had acted indifferent toward her, and the times he made love to her.

At that moment, Kelly finally admitted what she had been afraid to acknowledge: She was in love with Jake Cassidy, his cold arrogance, his stubbornness, his temper, his gentleness, and his passion. All that made him the man he was. No man had ever stirred her the way Jake did. But she knew now that it was more than physical attraction; it went much deeper than that. She wanted to be with him always, to assist Maureen in the running of the large house, to comfort Jake during the hard times and love him during the happy ones. To have his children and grow old beside him. That was what she wanted more than anything else.

Hearing a faint sound to her right, Kelly turned her head, able to see only a shadowy figure and the faint glow of a cigarette in the darkness. Obviously she wasn't the only one who couldn't sleep that beautiful night. When the dark figure turned, she could see Jake's face illuminated by the moonlight. He stood near a post, his eyes intent on her face. He slowly let the cigarette fall from his fingers and crushed it beneath his heel. She could see that his chest was bare except for the crisp dark hair covering it. Kelly couldn't keep her eyes from the virile man in front of her, unaware of the sensual, wraithlike picture she presented in her long nightgown and bare feet, with her hair loose about her shoulders.

Later, looking back, Kelly couldn't remember what happened to break the fragile spell, only that a soft sound escaped her throat as she flew down the veranda into Jake's arms. He crushed her against him, burying his face in her hair and inhaling the soft fragrance. His hands molded her body more completely against his.

"This is crazy," Jake muttered roughly, raining kisses over Kelly's face.

"I don't care. I don't care," she cried out joyfully, linking her arms around his neck. She gave herself up to his embrace, her new-found knowledge making her response that much more passionate.

"I can't sleep when all I do is dream of a beautiful woman with hair the shade of golden honey, eyes of polished turquoise." Jake stepped away from her and drew in a hissing breath, his eyes on Kelly's slightly parted lips. "A body made to be loved. A woman I want to be with."

Until now Kelly hadn't realized that a person could be seduced by words alone. But Jake was doing more than that. He was making love to her with his words and his eyes without even touching her.

Kelly's senses reeled as Jake took possession of her mouth again, his kiss hard and demanding, demanding a response she readily gave. The heat from his body scorched her through the thin material of her nightgown. Kelly was aware of a floating sensation as Jake picked her up in his arms, cradling her against his chest as she buried her face against his neck. Jake's long strides ate up the short distance to a set of open doors.

"I'm not going to let you go now," he muttered roughly.

Kelly was hazily aware of something soft yielding to her weight as Jake set her down. Bemused, she looked up at the man who could turn her to fire by his merest touch, cause her pulse to race with only a caressing glance. Kelly propped herself up on one elbow and held out her hand.

"Jake?" Her husky voice was questioning. He wouldn't leave her now, would he?

His dark face softened into a slow, sensual smile. He stretched out beside Kelly, drawing her into his arms and covering her with his body.

"Your hair smells like flowers." Jake's voice was muffled against her neck. He lifted his head to look directly into her eyes. The moonlight caused them to shimmer like two jewels. His hands momentarily tightened on her body, as if he were barely able to hold himself in check. "I want you, Kelly, but you know that, don't you? You're mine, and no one else can have you. And I know you want me."

"Yes." Her voice was a soft breath; she saw the look of open desire on Jake's face, and it frightened her. Kelly was aware of Jake's experience with women, but she had had no comparable experience with men. Would she be found wanting? Would he be disappointed in her? She wanted to please him so much.

"I wouldn't hurt you for the world, Kelly," he said softly, as if sensing her fears. The feathery touch of his lips against hers dissolved the last of her inhibitions. Her body moved instinctively against his, letting him know how much she wanted him. A moan escaped her lips.

Kelly was unaware that Jake had deftly removed her nightgown until she felt the sensuous touch of the soft linen sheets against her bare skin. All she wanted was his arms around her. She murmured a soft protest when he left her for a moment to strip off his own clothes. He laughed softly when Kelly's arms lifted toward him as he came back to her.

"You're all I want, Kelly James," he murmured to her. "All I need."

Her mind spun with bright lights. She was weightless, aware of nothing but Jake's hands and lips carrying her to new and dizzying heights. There couldn't be anything that could compare with these mindless feelings. Kelly's body was clay under Jake's touch. He was the sculptor creating her anew to suit him. Words were unnecessary between them. Something as beautiful and warm as their shared passion couldn't be ignored, and Kelly couldn't deny Jake anything. He had awakened a need in her, a need only he could fulfill. Her hands delighted in the feel of his warm, smooth skin as they glided over his muscular contours.

"We're alone on an island," Kelly whispered. "No one here but us."

Jake's soft laughter came from deep in his throat. "We don't need anyone else but each other. I only want you, Kelly James."

"I want to be yours, Jake. Yours only."

He drew back, looking at her face and seeing the rapture on her features. "I'll try not to hurt you, but . . ." he said huskily, "I seem to lose my mind when I'm with you."

Kelly smiled warmly. "Make love to me, Jake," she murmured.

Groaning, Jake's mouth descended hungrily on hers.

Then a steady, high-pitched buzzing cut through their shared passion. Jake swore fiercely under his breath as he switched on a nearby lamp. He picked up the telephone receiver, the scowl on his face promising doom to whoever had chosen this hour to call him.

"Cassidy," Jake growled into the receiver.

Kelly used her hand to shade her eyes against the bright light. As she surveyed her surroundings her brain suddenly cleared. This was Jake's bedroom, and she was in Jake's bed! Her body trembled in shock as she realized what could have happened if the phone hadn't rung just then. Jake would have made love to her in the fullest sense. Kelly's face burned with shame as she remembered her wanton response to Jake's lovemaking. From beneath the cover of her thick lashes she gazed covertly up at his scowling face as he spoke brusquely into the phone.

"Right, I'll take care of it." He replaced the receiver and turned his eyes to a still trembling Kelly. As if realizing that she was almost in a state of shock, he gathered her tenderly into his arms in a comforting gesture, his voice a low murmur in her ear.

"I—I feel so ashamed," Kelly whispered, refusing to look up at Jake's face. "I've never done anything like this. Ever."

"I know that, honey," he said gently. "Otherwise, I would have had you in my bed long ago."

Kelly shook her head in denial, feeling sobs gather in her throat. She felt so confused.

"Kelly, I don't want to, but I have to go." Jake's voice was tender. "One of my prize mares is foaling, and she's having trouble." His ragged breathing was evidence that he still hadn't regained all of his self-control.

"Please turn out the light," she begged. The bright light on the intimate scene made her feel cheap. Jake reached out, and a moment later the room was bathed in darkness, with only the moonlight spilling across the bed.

The bed shifted as Jake reluctantly put Kelly from him and got up, pulling on jeans and a cotton shirt. Kelly lay on her side with her back to him, her eyes blurred with tears. In the moonlit room Jake could see her tense, curled-up figure as he carefully pulled the covers over her. He sat on the edge of the bed, laying a hand on her bare shoulder as he dropped a light kiss on her hair. Biting her lower lip, Kelly shrugged Jake's hand away, wanting only to be alone with her confused thoughts.

"You did nothing to be ashamed of, honey," Jake said quietly. "You're a warm and desirable woman, capable of passion. And you have a beautiful gift. Don't deny yourself a love you deserve." Receiving no response, he rose to his feet and quietly let himself out of the room.

Kelly didn't turn even when she heard the sound of the door closing. She could see her nightgown lying on the carpet in a pool of moonlight. Tears stole down her cheeks, tears that soon turned into heavy, heartrending sobs, until she finally fell into an exhausted sleep.

Chapter Eight

When Kelly awoke, she could hear the muted sound of running water. Her eyes felt dry and itchy behind her closed eyelids. She slowly opened them, looking around with a puzzled frown at the unfamiliar surroundings. In a rush the events of the previous night came back to her.

Her head snapped up at the sound of a nearby door opening. Jake walked out of the bathroom clad in a heavy terry robe, his black hair still damp from his shower.

"Good morning." He flashed her a warm smile that reached all the way to his eyes.

"I—I'm sorry," Kelly mumbled as she pushed her hair away from her face. Suddenly realizing that she was nude under the sheet, she hastily drew it up to her chin. "I guess I fell asleep." The full import of her surroundings struck her. "What time is it?"

"Almost nine," Jake replied, adding, "I told Myrna that you were up earlier with a bad headache and had asked not to be disturbed." Walking toward the bed, he picked up Kelly's nightgown and handed it to her.

"How is the mare?"

"She had a beautiful, healthy filly," he said, with a trace of pride in his voice. "I figured I'd better come back for a shower and change of clothes." His eyes darkened to a deep emerald. "Kelly?" Jake's voice was husky with emotion, questioning.

"I—I can't Jake," she said in a low voice, looking very young and defenseless. "I just can't. I'm sorry."

Jake gazed down at her with all of his protective instincts raised. He thought that Kelly had never looked as beautiful as she did then, with sleep-flushed features and heavy eyes. He wanted nothing more than to lock the door and shut the world out, keeping her here with him. But the troubled expression in her turquoise eyes told him that he would only be rejected.

"I'll go out and make sure no one comes near this part of the house so you can slip back to your room." Jake walked toward the door. "The last I saw, everyone was out by the pool, so you shouldn't need to worry."

After Jake left, Kelly numbly reached for her nightgown and slipped it over her head. All she wanted now was to go to her room and hide her pain, pain because, although Jake had told her that he wanted to make love to her, he hadn't said that he loved her.

As the day wore on, Kelly's fictional headache became a harsh reality. She put on her green, one-piece bathing suit and headed for the pool, hoping that the sun would relieve the pounding in her temples.

Maureen and Susan were sitting by the pool

watching Billy and Sally play in the sun-warmed water. "Myrna mentioned that you had a headache earlier. How are you feeling?" Maureen asked sympathetically.

"I took some aspirin, so that should help." Kelly smiled faintly.

As she watched the children play in the water Kelly's spirits began to lift. Later, hearing men's voices, she looked up in dismay to see Jake and Pat coming out of the house wearing swimming trunks. Jake's eyes met Kelly's questioningly, but she hastily looked away, unable to face him.

Kelly took great care not to be alone with Jake for the remainder of the day. Myrna served lunch outside so they wouldn't have to worry about drying and changing their clothes. Kelly tied a floral print wrap skirt around her waist and made sure to sit next to Maureen during the meal to avoid any conversation with Jake.

"Much as I'd like to stay longer, I think we'll have to leave first thing in the morning," Pat told his mother.

Kelly's face showed no emotion, although shock flamed through her body. She knew she couldn't stay there without the protection of additional people. She had to leave without letting Jake find out ahead of time. He was a difficult man to say no to, and she knew he didn't want her to go just yet.

A short time after the meal, the men reentered the water to play ball with Billy.

"I think we have some lazybones around here." Pat hauled himself out of the pool and scooped up a squealing Susan in his arms. "Jake, you grab Kelly, and we'll throw them in."

Before Kelly could react, Jake had lifted her out of her chair. Her arms automatically curled around his neck as she remembered the last time he had picked her up in his arms.

"Perhaps I should drop you somewhere just as soft but much more private," Jake muttered for her ears only. "You didn't look so frightened then."

Kelly didn't answer, only stared at him with huge, startled eyes. She was so busy remembering their last encounter that she was totally unprepared when Jake's arms loosened, dropping her into the water. She surfaced spluttering and shaking her hair out of her eyes. Jake dove neatly into the water and swam over to Pat and Susan. Kelly immediately climbed out of the pool and took her towel over to a grassy spot and laid it out, stretching out on it to sun herself.

Perversely, Kelly now hoped that Jake would approach her, but he stayed away, seeming to prefer the company of his nephew and niece. Resting her cheek on her crossed arms, she closed her eyes and let the warm sun lull her into a drowsy state.

"Kelly?" She slowly turned over, blinking her eyes in confusion as she looked up into Maureen's smiling face. "We didn't want to disturb you until it was necessary."

"I guess I was more tired than I thought," Kelly said apologetically as she sat up. Her eyes encountered Jake's across the pool. He stood still, hands on hips, watching her with those soul-searching emerald eyes. "Ah, if you don't mind, I think I'll skip dinner and go to bed. I really don't have any appetite, anyway."

"Do you feel all right?" Maureen was immediately concerned as she laid the back of her hand against Kelly's forehead to check for a fever.

"It's just my headache," Kelly lied. "I think I'd feel better if I lay down." She stood up, taking her skirt off a nearby chair and tying it around her waist.

"Well, you should eat something. I'll bring you in some soup later."

Kelly went into the house, trying to stay as far away as possible from Jake. Inside the privacy of her room, she flopped onto the bed, working to collect her emotions.

"This is ridiculous," she muttered to herself. "I can't let anyone reduce me to this. I have to get away before it gets worse."

After a hasty shower Kelly slipped on a nightgown, knowing she'd have to play the part of an invalid. When she entered the bedroom, her eyes strayed toward the open doors leading to the veranda. She knew the room next to hers was empty, so the one past that had to be Jake's. She remembered the night she had woken up feeling as if someone were looking at her. Of course, it had been Jake! Running to the doors, Kelly hastily closed and locked them.

A short time later a soft knock sounded at the door and Maureen asked if she could come in. Kelly opened the door as the older woman entered, carrying a small tray.

"Myrna insists you finish the soup and tea," Maureen told her as she set the tray down on a nearby table. "I'm not trying to be an interfering mother, but did you and Jake have an argument after the party last night? You both seemed so tense with each other today."

Kelly choked back a hysterical laugh. "No, we didn't have an argument," she said quietly.

"I asked Jake and he nearly snapped my head off." Maureen put a hand on Kelly's shoulder. "Arguments can be very heartbreaking, Kelly. Your father and I found that out the hard way. I wouldn't want anyone to go through the agony I did."

Kelly impulsively hugged the older woman, feeling tears forming in her eyes. "I—I guess I'm just now beginning to find out about myself," she said huskily. "I need to make some very important decisions, and I feel at my wit's end."

"Knowing Jake, he'll try to barge in here like the proverbial bull in the china shop. I'll make sure to head him off." Maureen smoothed back Kelly's honey-blond hair. "A good night's rest will help put everything back in perspective. When you've finished your soup, just put the tray out by your door."

After Maureen had left, Kelly sat down at the small table to have her soup. After she finished her meal, she stood up and drew the drapes, preferring to feel shut in. Curling up on the bed with a book in her lap, she let her mind wander as the evening progressed. Once she heard Jake's voice, raised as if in anger, and Maureen's softer tones. A tear escaped Kelly's expressive eyes, then another, forming a trail down her cheeks and dampening her pillow. All of her life Kelly had always gotten what she wanted without thinking twice. Not that she had been spoiled by her parents and friends, but luck had always been on her side in anything she did. Until now. A tall, black-haired Australian with deep green eyes had changed all that. When she finally fell asleep, her head was pounding, and her sleep was dream-filled and restless as she tossed and turned in her bed.

When two hands gently gripped her shoulders, she shot up in bed, but her outcry was smothered as a hand swiftly covered her mouth.

"Don't be afraid. It's me—Jake," he whispered, sitting down next to her.

"What are you doing here?" Kelly demanded in a whisper. She turned her head to glance at the clock and saw that it was past two. "You're crazy to come here at this hour."

"And you're the one driving me there," Jake muttered. "My mother has been your faithful watchdog all evening. She informed me in no uncertain terms that I was not to disturb you."

"Then why are you here disturbing me now?"

"Because you disturb me," he said bluntly. "You disturb me a great deal. I want to know why you've been acting the way you have all day, as if you can't bear to have me touch you."

If you only knew the truth! Kelly thought hysterically to herself. She wanted Jake to touch her; she wanted that very much. With the moonlight spilling into the room they didn't need any artificial light to see each other's faces, Jake's taut and Kelly's distraught.

"Last night was a mistake," she said slowly, unable to look up at his face, afraid he'd read the real truth in her eyes. "If it hadn't been for that phone call, it would have been disastrous."

"Do you honestly believe that?" Jake demanded hoarsely.

"Yes."

Jake grabbed the hair at the nape of her neck, pulling her face upward, forcing her to look at him. "I don't believe you can say that again to my face." His emerald eyes glittered dangerously. "Because even with the anger I feel toward you right now, I still want to make love to you. And if you'd be honest enough to admit it to yourself, you want me, too." His other hand began a sensual exploration of Kelly's bare shoulder, dipping down beneath the low neckline of her nightgown to further explore her soft, responsive flesh.

"Don't, Jake," she said in a tortured whisper. She was painfully aware that her breathing had quickened under Jake's expert touch. She wanted to hate him for turning her world upside down, but she couldn't. She wanted to hate him for only desiring her physically, but she couldn't. She could only love him more each day.

"Don't deny yourself, Kelly," he murmured, bending his head to allow his lips to move along her throat. "We belong together. Don't you hear it? What our bodies are saying to each other? You can't deny it, Kelly. I can't, and I don't think you can, either."

"Oh, Jake." Hot tears pricked her eyelids. "It's all so wrong."

Jake's mouth moved upward to urgently cover hers, pressing her back against her pillow. "We need each other. And we need to talk," he muttered thickly, his breath mingling with hers. "Oh, Kelly, when I'm with you the last thing I want to do is talk." His hand warmly covering her breast brought back in a rush the memories of that night before the phone had interrupted them—and what would have happened if it hadn't. Kelly's own emotions smashed through all the barriers that she had put up between them.

"Then don't," she said breathlessly, lifting her lips, inviting his possession.

As Jake's mouth covered hers again, Kelly gave herself up to his caresses.

"Jake." Maureen's quiet voice penetrated the air.

Kelly pulled abruptly away from Jake's embrace, her face burning with shame as she saw the older woman standing quietly in the doorway.

"This has nothing to do with you, Mother," Jake said harshly.

"It has a great deal to do with me," she replied evenly. "I feel responsible for Kelly. Go to your room, Jake."

"You can't order me as if I were a child." His voice was harsh and savage.

"Leave us, Jake." There was a thread of steel in Maureen's soft voice. She didn't intend to be disobeyed.

Reluctantly Jake rose to his feet, keeping his eyes on Kelly's flaming face. Without a word to either woman, he left the room. Maureen entered, closing the door behind her.

"I feel so ashamed," Kelly whispered, unable to look up at Maureen.

"You shouldn't." The older woman sat down on the edge of the bed. "I know my son only too well. When he finally quieted down this evening, I knew he had a plan in mind. Nothing Jake does surprises me. He's made it quite clear that he wants you, and I'm aware that you also want him. I just wonder what the two of you will do about it."

Kelly could only shake her head, her hair shielding her face. She could feel the tears streaming down her face. Maureen put her arms around the younger woman's shoulders, comforting her as she would a child. It was a long time before Kelly fell asleep again.

The next morning Kelly had to rely on her skilled use of makeup to hide her red and puffy eyes. When she walked into the dining room, she was surprised to find everyone still there.

"How are you feeling, Kelly?" Pat looked up from his cup of coffee.

"Much better, thank you," she murmured, accepting a filled coffee cup from a blank-faced Jake.

"I'm just sorry we can't stay for a longer visit," Susan told her. "But, unfortunately, this time of year is very busy for Pat, so we've been lucky to get away for this long. We try to come for the Cup and the gala every year. I'm glad I got a chance to meet you, too. Too bad you're planning on leaving so soon." Her eyes slid questioningly in Jake's direction.

Kelly didn't reply, merely concentrating on her coffee instead.

An hour later Pat, Susan, and their children were on their way back to their home on the other side of the Cassidy land. Maureen and Kelly were walking slowly back to the house after seeing them off when Jake approached his mother with a pained expression on his face.

"There's an emergency at the summer camp," he said grimly, not looking at Kelly. "I'm going to throw a few things in a bag and fly out." Kelly knew that Acacia Tree had an airstrip and a small plane which, Jake had told her, was especially important during emergencies.

"How long will you be gone?" Maureen asked with concern.

"Three or four days, no longer than a week." He disappeared in the direction of the house.

Kelly walked over to the porch railing, looking out with unseeing eyes. A plan rapidly formed in her mind. With Jake gone, she could easily leave with no fear of a confrontation with him. She was still there looking out when Jake walked out of the house carrying a small canvas bag in one hand. Kelly turned, tensely clasping her hands together as Jake halted in front of her, looking down with equally tense features.

"If I didn't have to fly up to the summer camp, I wouldn't, believe me," Jake told her in a low voice. "We need to talk when I get back. It means a lot to me, Kelly."

"We don't have anything to talk about." She refused to look up at him.

Jake expelled a harsh breath of frustration at her words. He gripped her forearms, jerking her against him to receive his hard kiss before he released her so abruptly that she almost fell. Then he walked toward the Land-Rover, which he would drive down to the small airstrip where his plane was kept. He didn't look back as he drove off. Kelly swallowed the lump in her throat as she turned to go inside the house.

"You're going to leave today, aren't you?"

Startled, she looked up to find Maureen standing just inside the door. "I have to," Kelly said briefly.

The older woman's eyes were warm with compassion. "You're in love with Jake, aren't you?" Kelly nodded, her eyes brimming with tears. "If so, why are you leaving?" Maureen asked gently. "Have you told him that you love him?"

"No, I haven't, because he needs someone

who was brought up around here to share his life, someone he loves. I wouldn't fit in, and he'd end up hating me for it," she said shakily. She raised eyes full of entreaty. "I have to leave. Please understand."

"Will Jake?"

Kelly could only shake her head as she ran past the older woman. "He'll go after you," Maureen called after her.

"No, no, he won't," Kelly choked out.

Kelly was able to book a seat on the next day's flight to Sydney. It was difficult for her to say goodbye to Maureen after all the kindness the older woman had shown her. Maureen alternately argued and pleaded with Kelly to stay until Jake returned, but that was one point Kelly was firm on.

The following day Kelly was in a hotel in Sydney. Calling the airport, she booked a reservation on a flight to the States leaving the next afternoon. Unable to eat dinner that evening, she went to bed early and fell asleep with tears on her cheeks. Her sleep was fitful and filled with dreams of Jake.

The next afternoon Kelly entered the airport terminal, oblivious to the admiring male glances she received. Dressed in an apricot-colored linen skirt and vest with a striped silk shirt and her honey-colored hair twisted up on top of her head, she outwardly resembled the composed young woman who had arrived in Australia six weeks earlier. Inwardly, she knew she would never be the same again. Jake had seen to that. Standing in line at the check-in counter, Kelly impatiently tapped the toe of one dark brown suede shoe, wanting only to board the jet and get far away from memories of the Australian drawl she heard all about her.

"Oh!" Kelly gasped suddenly as a steel vise gripped her wrist and pulled her out of line, dragging her toward the terminal doors. "What are you doing?" she demanded of her captor.

"What do you *think* I'm doing?" Jake bit out the words from between clenched teeth.

Kelly found that her high heels were a hazard as Jake pulled her along without looking back. Once she stumbled and would have fallen if she hadn't grabbed his arm to steady herself. Jake halted abruptly, looking down at her confused face.

"Oh, Kelly, why do you do this to me?" he groaned, cradling her face between his palms as his mouth hungrily and urgently descended on hers; he seemed to be totally uncaring of the fact that they were in a public place.

Kelly's blood raced under Jake's touch. Oblivious to the passersby in the busy terminal, Jake continued to kiss her as if they were alone and had all the time in the world. When he finally lifted his head, he flashed her a crooked grin. "As we're collecting an audience here, I think we'd better go somewhere with a little more privacy." Jake's hand retained its grip on Kelly's wrist, although more gently, as they walked outside. Still under the spell of Jake's kiss, Kelly could only follow numbly until sanity returned to her.

"My—my luggage!" she protested, gesturing back toward the terminal.

Jake muttered something uncomplimentary about Kelly's luggage. "You won't need it," he said grimly, pushing her none too gently into a nearby taxicab as he gave the driver the name of a well-known hotel.

"How did you know where I was?" Kelly fixed him with an accusing stare as the answer dawned on her. "Maureen! She told you, didn't she?"

"She contacted me on the radio right after you left. I've been hanging around the airport ever since, checking all the flights leaving for New York." Jake's expression was bleak when he turned to her. "Why, Kelly?"

She looked up at his face, wishing she could wipe away the lines of tension she saw there. "I'd stayed longer than I expected to," Kelly replied evasively. "It was time for me to leave."

Jake's eyes flickered toward the taxi driver's back and he let the subject drop.

"Please let me out, Jake," Kelly begged. "I'm going to miss my plane."

Jake continued to ignore her pleas as the taxi traveled through town. He sat back and closed his eyes, as if finally allowing his tense muscles to relax. Kelly couldn't keep her eyes off him; he was clad in tan slacks and a dark brown shirt which accented the dark tan of his face.

When the taxi pulled up in front of the hotel, Jake paid the driver and helped Kelly out, all the while keeping a firm grip on her arm. He had apparently checked in here when he got to Sydney, because he pulled her directly across the large lobby to the elevators. When they reached their floor, Jake pulled Kelly down the hallway without ceremony. Her face burned with embarrassment as an older couple watched them curiously.

"One little argument and you think you can call the honeymoon off and run home to Mother," Jake drawled for their benefit as he stopped in front of a door and pulled a key out of his pants pocket. He thrust Kelly inside the room and kicked the door shut behind him.

With maddening casualness Jake leaned back against the door, crossing his arms in front of his chest as he blocked off any escape. "Now, are you going to tell me why you really took off that way without a word or even a goodbye?"

"I said goodbye to your mother." Kelly looked around the tastefully decorated suite. An open door revealed a large bedroom completely dominated by a king-sized bed.

"That isn't what I meant." Jake's eyes glittered dangerously. "What are you running away from, Kelly James?"

"Jake, I'm going to miss my plane," she said, desperate to put as much distance as possible between them.

He straightened and advanced slowly toward a wary and wide-eyed Kelly. "You're a liar," Jake murmured, amusement lacing his husky voice. "You don't want to leave here."

"Yes, I do," she insisted, though without conviction.

Jake's hand gripped the back of Kelly's head as he stopped directly in front of her.

"Please don't, Jake," she pleaded. "Haven't you tormented me enough?"

"Not as much as you've tormented me," he muttered, his mouth scant inches above hers, tantalizing her with its nearness. "All I can think about is that night I had you in my bed and how you felt in my arms. The way your hair smells like flowers and your skin's as soft as silk. I can still taste your kisses; they can be very addicting. If Rick hadn't called, you would have been mine body and soul that night without any reservations on your part. I want you back in my bed, Kelly. Kissing me, caressing me, loving me."

"Noooo," she moaned, trying to twist her head away but unable to evade his grasp.

Jake's eyes narrowed to emerald slits. "At least your father had the grace to send a letter. You weren't even going to do that, were you? Just walk out and not look back. Perhaps, later on, you'd think with an amused laugh about that cattle rancher in Australia. I'd be an anecdote for your friends in New York. Is that more your style?"

"No! And what do you care, anyway?" Kelly asked miserably. "Sheila would do just as well for you if I wasn't around. You don't need me."

Jake's thumb probed the corner of her mouth, teasing her lips. "Sheila wasn't the reason I was so hard on Rick that night he called me," he said in a low voice. "And Sheila isn't the woman I love, the woman I want to marry and share my life with. To have my children. I wouldn't come after Sheila the way I came after you, you can be sure of that. I love *you*, Kelly, not Sheila."

"What?" Kelly looked up with disbelief. "You—you *love* me?"

"You crazy female," Jake groaned, pulling her against him. "Of course I love you. I decided you were what I was looking for the first time I saw you that day in your hotel room. It tore my guts out when you let me think Kyle was your lover. I figured then that you weren't the woman I thought you were, but it didn't stop me from falling in love with you, wanting you and hating myself for it at the same time. When I realized how innocent you really were, I could have jumped for joy, because I knew then that you were meant for me, after all."

Kelly clung to Jake's shoulders for fear her legs wouldn't support her. His hungry kiss told her much more effectively than words could how he felt about her. Jake pulled her shirt out of the waistband of her skirt, his hand moving sensually up her bare spine and arching her body closer to his.

"I told my mother I wasn't coming back until I had made you my wife," he muttered. "We'll apply for the license tomorrow, and I'm not going to let you out of my sight until you're legally mine. I'm not going to lose you again."

"But what about the problem at the summer camp you had to fly up to take care of?"

"I called Pat. He can take care of it." Jake dismissed her arguments.

"I have to return to New York," Kelly said weakly. "There are business negotiations, and Kyle; I'll have to explain to Kyle."

"Then we'll honeymoon there," Jake said arrogantly, adding hesitantly, "I never thought to ask you if your career means a great deal to you. Do you want to continue it? The Outback is pretty lonely, without much to offer someone used to the life you've always had."

Kelly cupped her palm against his cheek, looking up at him with loving eyes. "Oh, Jake, you mean so much more to me than any career. I'm just so glad that you feel the same way about me. Especially now that you've forced me to miss my plane. Oh, no!" She clapped her hand over her mouth. "My luggage had already been put on the plane. I don't have any clothes to wear."

"As far as I'm concerned, you won't be needing them for a while." Jake's caresses were creating strange sensations all up and down Kelly's spine. He looked down at her flushed features, his eyes a deep emerald with barely controlled passion. "This suite has two bedrooms. You can have your choice."

Kelly smiled, looking up at the man who had captured her heart and would soon be her husband and lover for all time. Her arms linked around his neck as she arched her body invitingly against his.

"Well, you did say you weren't going to let me out of your sight, didn't you?" she asked provocatively.

6 brand new Silhouette Special Editions yours for 15 days–Free!

For the reader who wants more...more story...more detail and description...more realism...and more romance...in paperback originals, 1/3 longer than our regular Silhouette Romances. Love lingers longer in new Silhouette Special Editions. Love weaves an intricate, provocative path in a third more pages than you have just enjoyed. It is love as you have always wanted it to be—and more —intriguingly depicted by your favorite Silhouette authors in the inimitable Silhouette style.

15-Day Free Trial Offer

We will send you 6 new Silhouette Special Editions to keep for 15 days absolutely free! If you decide not to keep them, send them back to us, you pay nothing. But if you enjoy them as much as we think you will, keep them and pay the invoice enclosed with your trial shipment. You will then automatically become a member of the Special Edition Book Club and receive 6 more romances every month. There is no minimum number of books to buy and you can cancel at any time.

Silhouette Romance

Coming next month from
Silhouette Romances

Logic Of The Heart by Dixie Browning

Emma was looking forward to seeing the romantic island of Hatteras, and meeting Dan Slater added to the magic. She could see herself slipping into his arms and falling under his spell. . . .

Devil's Bargain by Elaine Camp

Was Alexis being caught up in an evil scheme or was Drayce's renewed love for her genuine? Their once passionate marriage seemed too distant to recapture those lost moments of ecstasy. Yet suddenly Drayce made Alexis forget why escape was so important!

Flight To Romance by Tracy Sinclair

Jennifer was not going to refuse Kalim Al Kahira, when he asked her to return with him to Egypt. She told herself her career demanded that she go—until she realized that there was no way to refuse his dark, penetrating eyes.

In Name Only by Roxanne Jarrett

Jill traveled to Brazil to enter into an arranged marriage. She was determined not to be ruled by her new husband, but soon she found herself unable to deny the mad passions that filled her with desire.

Sweet Surrender by Donna Vitek

Suzanne's trip to Italy turned out to be anything but the quiet visit she anticipated. For once she met Jared Caine she felt compelled to compete for his attention and show him the depth and breadth of her love.

The Second Time by Janet Dailey

Dawn returned home to the Florida Keys to seek peace in the turquoise waters. But soon calm waters are turned into turbulent seas when passions are ignited by her old flame Slater MacBride.

READERS' COMMENTS ON SILHOUETTE ROMANCES: